FROM TIM

CHAPTER ONE

The year is 1935. Cold winds from the Pacific whistle through Everett, Washington. Shivering bees buzz inside a dry hive woven to the bark of a bald cypress. Family and friends stepping and stomping around the alabaster dwelling near the water bank have awakened the winter nesters, who burrow into one another. Inside the brick home, guests scuffle about as they haul furniture and other household items. Emma Wexford kneels to tie brown paper bags of cotton around a large, antique mirror. She smiles as her grey-haired mother playfully pokes Henri with an ornate fork as the two wrap and pack sterling silverware along with Japanese porcelain.

Emma stands up and stretches her back, yawning.

Heading through the foyer, she passes dark mahogany columns, painstakingly hand-engraved with an Italian scroll motif and then steps onto a Persian rug of violet, indigo, and cerise. Immediately, two of her neighbors pause in their preparation to roll up the rug across the white marble floor. Emma steps back with a smile. Both neighbors smile—one tipping his pale-green boater hat—before flipping the rug into a bundle.

"Pardon us, Miss Emmeline."

"Oh hush, Richard!" Emma responds laughing. "Your help needs no apology."

A quirky smile springs across Richard's face as he and his mate hoist the rug onto their shoulders.

Emma continues past walls where ivory décor and rococo paintings in heavy gilt frames play tug-of-war with her eyes. Not having bothered to lace her outfit with a belt that morning, her button-shirt with a cream blouse and cloud-grey bottom now hangs loosely about her waist. Soft blond hair waves freely down to the small of her back.

Emma's best friend from secondary school, Sarah March—with somber brown hair but impish kelly-green eyes—passes by with a light-blue vase filled with roses, yellow daisies, and rosemary. As the aromatic fragrance wafts in the air, Emma pauses to close her eyes and inhale deeply.

"Oh, don't throw those away yet! Set them here," she instructs, pointing to the nearest corner of the room. "I will take care of that in the morning."

Sarah smiles and sets the vase down snug in the corner, "Now don't keep yourself from visiting just because you're moving. You are the only person I can stand in this town."

Emma laughs, "Oh, I will visit so often it will be like I never left. And hush, you have your husband."

Sarah raises her eyebrows, "Yes, and still, you are the only person I can stand in this..."

Emma pinches her friend, trying not to laugh.

Sarah touches her arm and giggles.

"This Sunday, Em, I best see you." Sarah looks back at Emma as she turns to walk away.

"This Sunday," Emma confirms.

Suddenly, the corner of her eye catches her father and his friends moving her glistening black grand piano through the front double-doors.

"Father, please lift something not so heavy!" Emma cries as she races toward him.

Before she can reach her father, the piano breaches the open double doors. Without responding, Emma's father lifts the piano higher, sweating profusely. She watches with her hands clasped together tightly as the men waddle with the awkward instrument down the red brick porch-steps and along the path to a black iron gate.

"Be careful!" Emma stands in the doorway, which opens to a panorama of vibrant azaleas bordering the impeccably manicured front yard. Rabbiteye blueberry bushes, wilting from the weight of berries leftover from the plucking months of late summer, line both sides of the path. Between the porch and the gate, the path forms a circle around a white fountain. Stone cupids dance around a colossal dolphin as it spouts clean water all over their wings.

Relinquishing with a sigh after her father and piano reach their destination safely, Emma returns to the foyer. Her hair lifts from her shoulders as a breeze blows through three open windows, each of which stretch from the floor to the twenty-foot ceiling. Through the apertures, she sees Lake Stevens, whose waters mirror almost magically the earthy tree line along its banks as far as the eye can see. The glass triplets also allow the sun to shed unadulterated light through the foyer and into the kitchen where two rustic aqua dressers wait to be moved as they guard malachite countertops. Laughter and orders fill the air as loved ones carry the contents of her home outside and into the brisk October morning. Tomorrow, she moves into a smaller home on the lake east of Everett.

Upon reaching the top of the stairwell, Emma continues down the hall and into the master bedroom, shutting the door behind her with a thud. She inhales the silence. Twisting and rubbing her neck, Emma steps toward her bed but notices the wardrobe door cracked open with unpacked clothes and shoes. She glances back over at her bed covered with layers of thick, downy satin sheets which beckon her beneath a carved, gleaming, ebony headboard that once took six men to haul up the stairs. Sighing in resignation, she turns and walks inside her wardrobe. She reaches up and begins to dismantle dresses and coats of many fine fabrics—vicuña wool and charmeuse silk —and lays them with care in a leather trunk.

Kneeling to gather a pair of red French dress shoes, Emma notices a small jewelry box tucked under some silk shirts. She swallows hard.

"Oh, how could I forget!"

She sets the rose-colored shoes down and digs under the shirts, pulling the box into the light. Holding it tenderly, she draws the box to her chest and leans back as memories flood her mind like water through a broken dam. She turns the box around slowly, remembering its beautiful color during a time before the sea-green paint began to fade and peel. Her fingertips study the oxidized steel edges and follow its twists into little swirls that form small handles. She admires the piece for several minutes. Then a sad smile spreads across her face, and she slowly opens the top drawer. She reaches in and stares at what her hands now cradle with care—a leaf.

The lifeless flora, brittle with age, retains a faint, red, unnatural stain on the underside which is nearly faded away completely. It suggests writing that has become illegible through decay. Covering her mouth with one hand, Emma recites the words from memory while soft tears paint her cheeks. As the last words from the crinkled leaf leave her lips, her thoughts escape and run backward to the year 1912, to where it began.

***

A forceful knocking at the front door turns a man's head as he sits in a spacious brick house at the end of a cul-de-sac. Each home in the neighborhood is separated from the next by a fair span of distance.

"Hello-o!" a young voice rings from outside. The man in the home, Mr. Wexford, is one who looks down upon people in conversation. He stands, while twisting his grey handlebar mustache, and opens the door to find a young boy standing as tall as possible on the front porch. Eleven-year-old Emma peeks around her bedroom door from the top of the stairs. The boy is of good stock and average height for an eleven-year-old. He wears a pair of pressed tan pants and a sporty-looking navy jacket to keep the cool North Pacific wind at bay. His dark wavy hair piles thick atop his head while his feet flaunt a pair of brown dress shoes which, from the sight of them, seem like old hand-me-downs that he hasn't quite grown into yet. The boy must have heard the door open, but he remains looking down at a sheet of paper in his hand. Mr. Wexford examines the child for a moment and notices a wagon of flowers parked on the walk side.

Mr. Wexford asks abruptly, "What is it I can do for you, lad?"

"Oh, Good mornin'!" the boy answers, with enough force to knock over a horse. "Are you the father of the home here?"

Mr. Wexford smiles. "Yes sir, now what can I do for you?"

"Just need a minute of your time, sir. My name is Tim Anderson. I am the one who has been 'round the neighborhood sittin' down with the families to show fresh roses for Valentines which is at two days 'way. You wouldn't by chance have a special lady in your life with whom you will be celebratin' Valentine's Day with, would you?"

Mr. Wexford opens the door wider and nods at the boy. "So, you're selling flowers?"

Grinning with pride after saying his rehearsed pitch perfectly, Tim replies, "Yes sir, I happen to be. The best Washington has to offer up, I believe. I have only a few minutes of time to show them, too;

wouldn't want the mother of the house walking in while you are selecting her roses. That'd just 'bout ruin the whole lot now, wouldn't it?"

Tim turns and bounds down the front porch steps to the wagon, scoops up some flowers, and races back up to Mr. Wexford, who is checking his pocket watch. "Step inside, Tim. My wife is away, and we can sit down and look at these flowers of yours."

"Thank you, sir." Tim wipes his shoes on the mat and enters the house. He sits down on one of two brown leather couches, opposite from Mr. Wexford. Immediately, Tim begins handing over different colorful bouquets, explaining their differences in form and match.

While Mr. Wexford looks over the flowers, Tim notices a half-full cup of tea in a fine-China dish left next to a yellow book plopped open on the coffee table. Sewn into the spine with black thread, still shining with gloss, is the title *Germinal*. The pages, stiff, have only been turned to page 3. Tim's eyes follow the opened front cover of the book which points to a cross-legged Mr. Wexford, whose brown leather shoes gleam. The shoes house steel-grey socks, rising high on Mr. Wexford's ankles and disappearing beneath his midnight blue pants. His belt, almost as ridged as the hardwood floor, locks tightly about his waist. A vanilla-colored dress shirt paints the man from wrist to neck and a maroon sweater vest wraps snug down to his hips. Tim suspects that these soft clothes show this was the man's day off, but that he still dressed presentably, as if his work ethic spilled over into his leisure time. Tim sees a man struggling to control his thoughts and emotions, so he chooses to control everything else around him.

The crackling fire and apple-cider scent of the tea tempts Tim to relax for a moment, but he quickly shakes his mind loose from the thought. Tim offers, "My preference is for the white roses with yellow daisies; those are my mother's favorite."

"Where do you pluck these, lad? They are quite green for this time of year."

"I pluck them from Sanford's Flowers on the other side of the block. Mr. Sandford lets me go door-to-door and sell them for 'im every year."

After looking over the different flower sets for a while, Wexford hands back every bouquet except the one with white roses and yellow daisies. "Well, I don't know Mr. Sandford, but you may go back and tell him Robert Wexford says he certainly is a pundit when it comes to raising roses. I like these, and I will take them. What's your price?"

"I will, sir! And it is only a pair of jitneys for those."

Wexford extracts two coins from a small purse and drops them into Tim's cupped palm. Tim sifts the change in his oily hand before proudly putting it in his pocket.

Standing to leave, Tim shakes Mr. Wexford's engulfing grip as firmly as he is able. "Thank you, sir. Have any questions you'd like to ask before I skip?"

Robert Wexford holds back a smile as he responds to the young entrepreneur. "Yes, I am curious as to how your sales are persisting?"

"They are goin' well, sir. So long as you keep positive, people usually buy."

"Well, I am glad to hear it." Wexford displays a slight grin. "I imagine you get quite a share of doors slammed on you."

Tim grins, "Only all day, sir!"

Wexford laughs as he walks his new acquaintance to the door. Tim continues, "The people who have just moved to Everett usually hand me the hardest time, so I thank you."

Wexford, with a full smile, says, "Why, yes, it happens my family and I finished moving into this home yesterday. The view across Lake Stevens is absolutely positive. My daughter Emma starts her first day at the Everett Elementary upon the morrow."

Curious, Emma listens at her door. She sticks her head out and briefly makes eye contact with Tim from upstairs. Tim, ready to respond to Mr. Wexford, catches her stare and freezes. His momentary stun soon elapses, allowing his face to harden back to the countenance he had before he became lost in the pair of Emma's bluebird-blue eyes, before his jaw fell slightly ajar.

Emma's cheeks flush red. She yanks her head back into her room, slamming her door abruptly. Mr. Wexford turns his gaze swiftly towards the top of the stairs. He lets out a simple "hmf" and then turns back to Tim.

"Well, perchance I will meet her, sir," Tim says as he glances up towards Emma's door. "That school down the street is the one I attend. Have a wonderful mornin'!"

"Now you be careful, lad," Wexford says as Tim leaps down the steps and speeds his wagon away to the next house.

Mr. Wexford closes the front door just as Emma leaves her room.

"Daddy, who was that?"

"His name was Tim, Emmy. I bought some flowers from him for Mother." Wexford pulls the bouquet up to show his daughter.

"Oh, they are pretty! Mommy will be quite fond of them."

"I think she will too." He admires the flowers briefly before strolling to the kitchen in search of something to put them in.

Emma waits.

She then runs to the front door and looks down the street. She scans the new neighborhood of copper-red brick homes and light green lawns bedecked with waist-high, brown fences. The fences provide feigned guardianship of Douglas fir and spruce trees waving long, healthy branches. Emma's eyes take in the grey-bluish sky full of puffy, ashen clouds hovering just above the heavily hilled range. The smell creeping up and permeating the air tells her that rain is about to fall.

Emma sees a few women in friendly conversation on the front porch next door, swaying on a crackled white swing-bench. The neighbors wear white gowns with floral designs. They hold stark red teacups and saucers as they sip and chit-chat. At the end of the street, construction workers in thick boots swing harmers to nails on the roof of a new house.

The cold February weather quietly steals the warmth from Emma's home as the door remains open. She looks as far as her eyes let her, but she cannot see the boy. Stepping back to shut the door, she finds a white rose lying across the doormat. Wide-eyed, she picks it up, shuts the door, and runs with it upstairs to her room. Tim, peeking from behind a tree, smiles.

***

"Timmy! Time to get u-up!"

Tim's eyes pop open and he hops out of bed. "I'm up! I'm up!" He runs in peach boxer-shorts to his dresser and rustles through the drawers. The top drawer has socks, the next drawer holds white undershirts, and the bottom drawer has fresh underwear, none of which are folded. Tim snags an article from each drawer, dropping a sock to the floor in the process, and runs to the shower.

Turning the brass knob, he shivers as cold water splashes over his body. He bathes quickly. As he steps out of the tub, he smells the crude-cut strips of bacon his mother is frying on an iron skillet in the kitchen.

Standing in front of the mirror, Tim furrows his brows, forming a stern face while using his fingers to comb his curly hair. He tilts his chin up and rubs the soft fuzz on his face—still a few more years until he needs shaving cream. Raising his wiry arms, he crunches his abdominals. Tim stands too close to the mirror, which only reflects his head and chest. He steps backward and flexes again, smiling while checking himself out in different poses.

Suddenly his eyes widen as he remembers the reason for his excitement this morning. He throws on a pair of khaki pants, a dark green dress shirt, and the brown shoes he wore the day before.

"Timmy! Breakfast!" his mother shouts.

"Coming!"

His mother set down a steaming plate of fluffy scrambled eggs next to the bacon he smelled. She sticks the eggs with a three-pronged fork and fills a glass with water from a slightly cracked pitcher, plopping two cubes of ice into the glass. She always keeps a tray filled with sink-water in the icebox.

Tim creeps down the hallway and peeks around the corner. He watches his mother wrap a salami sandwich in a blue napkin. She places it in a bulky orange lunchbox along with an apple. The lunchbox flattens a curling flap on the beige kitchen counter that often peels up revealing the glue beneath. On a hook by the side of the sink hangs a wet blue kitchen rag. A tin trash can stands below the towel where thudding drops of water drip into. Tim's mother placed the can there to protect the floor from growing mold.

The living room floor is dark beige carpet. A navy-blue sofa in the center of the room faces a small brown brick fireplace that funnels up into a narrow chimney. Four tiny oval frames nailed into the walls show black and white photos—one of a Union soldier with a thick beard; one with a formal family portrait of a mother, father, and a newborn boy wrapped in a blanket; one of a one-story, two-bedroom home taken from the street; and the last with a Native American holding a spear in one hand and a beaver pelt in another. Two photos adorn each side of the chimney.

Tim runs through the living room, ducking. He almost makes it to the front door.

"Adam Timothy Anderson!"

He stops. "Mom, I do not have time for breakfast this morning! I really need to get to school!"

She grabs his lunch box and holds it out in front of him. "And is your schedule so busy that you gotta get git' without your lunch and starve in the afternoon?"

Tim lets out a groan. As he reaches for his lunchbox, his mother places it on top of the refrigerator. "Sit and eat your breakfast."

He grimaces and looks at the clock hanging on the kitchen wall. His mother sits down at the round kitchen table and salts her food. She is a youthful forty-year-old woman with smile-wrinkles and reddish-brown hair, except for a few grey strands. A rose-red string ties her hair back, showing her prominent forehead and narrow eyebrows. Her skin is soft, especially atop her hands where periwinkle veins appear.

Tim walks over to his plate, grabs his fork, and shovels eggs into his mouth, stuffing his cheeks with a second bite before he has swallowed the first. His mother sets the salt down. "Goodness! What is your hurry today? I'm usually beating on your door by now still trying to get you out of bed."

"Eif haff touf geh touf schoo eree," he responds through a mouthful of eggs.

His mother turns her head and covers her eyes with her hands. "Please swallow that."

Tim swallows hard and then gulps down his water, slamming the empty cup on the table, panting. "I have to get to school early." Wiping his mouth, he gives his mother a kiss on the cheek.

She smiles. "Brush those pearls before you leave."

Running back to his bathroom, he smells his breath through a cupped palm. With his toothbrush full of paste, he scrubs every bit of surface in his mouth, being sure to get the back of his tongue, then gargles and spits into the sink.

Tim runs through the kitchen, grabs his lunch, opens the door and bounds down the steps shouting, "Love you!" as the door slams behind him.

A rising sun peeks above the horizon. The moisture of fog sticks to Tim's face and wind presses his clothes against his skin. The air is cool, and the scent of dewy grass floats up from the front lawn. Tim rushes down the street to meet his waiting friends.

"Seven a.m. sharp, Tim. What a miracle you made it out on time. We were just about to leave you... again." David Peace is Tim's oldest comrade, having known each other since they were both learning to walk.

"The early bird gets the worm, Dave," Tim responds.

"Yeah, but the second rat gets the cheese, Timbo," rebuts Charlie Smith, a pudgy boy whose family moved up from the South a couple years before.

"Always thinking about food, huh?" Dave blurts out.

"Another joke about my size? How about you make an original jab for once," Charlie responds.

"I'd knock you out flat as wood if I hit you with these pipes," Dave says while flexing his arms.

"Well hey, that cheese will be the first rat's if he is faster! Let's hurry ourselves!" Tim commands as he takes off.

"It's too early to be runnin' to school. I just woke up." Charlie says.

"I know," Tim answers. He slows down, his face red with embarrassment. "I just don't want to walk in tardy," he lies. "Mrs. White moved annoyin' Becky to the front and I don't want to be stuck with a seat by her. That's all."

"True as that is, I don't feel like runnin' to school, I ain't no nerd," says Charlie.

"Besides, if that happens," David adds, "we can just toss a bug on Becky's desk and get her to run out of class like last year!"

Charlie laughs and Tim smiles slightly; his mind is still on another matter.

As they turn the last corner to get to school, the three friends see two familiar boys heading to school on the other side of the street. "What a dark day. Look at the mole and his dog over there," David mutters.

John Calhoun is walking with his oversized companion, Brad Hum. John's family is wealthy from an inheritance on his father's side. His slicked back strawberry blond hair smells like a perfumery. He is frail, and wears a plastic smile that one could purchase at a local corner store. Hum, on the other hand, is a large boy, both fat and muscular. He has pale skin and tough hands and a mother who is careful to feed him or else deal with his short temper.

"I would sure like to catch Calhoun without Hum around. I'd put a hurt on him that even his Dad's dough couldn't buy him out of," Charlie says, spitting on the ground. Tim nods in agreement but remains quiet.

As they approach the school, Tim challenges eagerly, "Hey, guys, the school is right there! Bet I can beat you in!" He takes off quickly, not noticing that Charlie and David continue to just walk.

Charlie scrunches his face. "What's up with Timbo?"

"It has got to be all those flowers he sells. I keep tellin' him that if you sniff them enough your mind goes crazy. He might even get sent home for being sick now." David shakes his head. "That's a dratted shame, too, 'cause we studied all Sunday for the mathematics test today."

Charlie stops in his tracks. "We've got a test today? Well, ain't a one told me that! I ain't study a bit for it! Tell me you is just yanking on me, Dave? We don't really have no test?"

"We sure do. I tell's ya to pay attention in class," scolds David.

Charlie rips a handful of flowers from under a nearby bush and smells them intensely until the two friends enter the school.

Tim arrives in the classroom panting and searching every face of his chattering classmates. He sees boys with buttoned-up shirts, creased knickers and neatly combed hair. Girls sit cross-legged in high-collared blouses and long skirts. A few stiff chairs are occupied while others remain vacant or accompanied by a boy sitting on the wooden desk that the teacher repeatedly asserts is used "for writing on, not sitting on." Tim looks everywhere but to no avail, so he walks languidly to the back of the room. His chair screeches the floor as he plops in it.

David and Charlie walk in soon after. Charlie still sniffs the handpicked rhododendrons. David grabs the flowers. "Blazes, Charlie! You are goin' to take the test today!" Then he throws them in the garbage. Charlie pouts, which David ignores. The two join Tim in the back of the classroom.

Tim glances at the clock as the hours go by. After each class, he hopes she will show up, but by the last class of the day he stops looking at the clock altogether.

"Perhaps she's not my year," he mutters under his breath as he stares at the floor. He releases a sigh, but then looks up. His eyes widen and a smile spreads between his cheeks. Emma, arriving so late to class as to nearly miss school completely, nervously walks into the classroom with a lost look on her face. She sits at the desk in front of Tim as the teacher prepares to lecture on the blackboard. Tim's heart thuds in his chest.

A white ribbon ties Emma's silky blond tresses into a ponytail. To Tim, Emma's hair begs to be touched. Her cotton-pink shoes complement the pink dress she wears. She holds her books tightly against her chest as she sits silently, fidgeting and crossing her ankles.

The class soon winds down and the school day comes to a close. The teacher ends his lecture while Tim is lost in reverie, trying to figure out how he will introduce himself to the girl just an arm's length away. He daydreams about her until the bell rings and class ends. Emma stands up to leave. Tim's body jerks like he's received a splash of ice water in the face. Charlie and David approach, but Tim stands up and pushes them away without a word. They give each other a look. Dave answers, "Alright bud, see ya outside."

The children chatter as they pack up to leave. Louder than he'd wanted to, Tim blurts, "Emma!"

Emma's shoulders jump, and she spins around to see who called her name. She sees Tim and answers, "Yes?"

"Hi there," Tim stutters.

In a shy voice, Emma responds, "Hello."

Tim wipes his sweaty hand on his leg and then extends it. "My name is Adam. That's my first name, but you can call me Tim, or Timothy. Most of my friends just call me Tim. Tim is my middle name. Well, really, Timothy is, but Tim is short for that. My last name is Anderson. You can call me what you want, though!" Tim knows he has said too much.

Emma lights up and turns pink. "Pleased to meet you, Tim." She reaches out and shakes his clammy hand.

"First day?" Tim asks, trying to keep the conversation going.

"It is," Emma responds, looking at the ground.

"Well, humdinger!" Tim begins winding his fingers together.

"Thank you," Emma says. There is a pause. After a moment, she smiles politely at Tim and turns to leave. Tim blurts out, "Will you have me as a valentine?"

She turns to face him once more. They are the only two left in the classroom. "What do you mean?"

"Oh, I ask if you want to be a valentine with me! You understand, for Valentine's Day tomorrow?" Tim is shaking.

"Well, what does a valentine *do*?" Emma tilts her head and smiles.

Relieved not to be refused, Tim explains, "Valentines are two people who like each other on Valentine's Day! I'm venturin' to see if you want to be my valentine. I get to be your valentine too, if you'd like."

"Oh..." Emma glances away, squeezing her books tighter. He blushes, awaiting her answer.

Looking back at him, she answers. "You and I

are not familiar, though."

Tim grins. "That I can fashion! We'll get to be familiar, no problem."

"And how do we do that?"

"Um, my favorite color is green. What 'bout yours?" Tim asks.

"Red," she answers.

"There, now we are familiar," he states proudly.

She looks him in the eye and smiles. "Very well. Are the other kids going to have valentines tomorrow?"

"They are!"

"Well in that case, yes," Emma says.

"Yes what?"

"Yes, I will be your valentine."

"Oh! Drat, I knew that. Sorry, I thought you meant 'yes' to another matter!" Tim lies nervously.

"Very well, I will see you tomorrow!" Emma turns to leave.

"Goodbye, Emma!" They walk home separately that day, Emma with butterflies in her stomach and Tim with his head held high.

CHAPTER TWO

The next day both the students and the teachers enjoy a school draped from top to bottom in Valentine's Day decorations. Bright pastel hearts with white paper doilies stick to the walls and little nude cupids with wings and bows are plastered everywhere. The smell of sweet, sugary candy fills the hallways, and laughter comes from nearly every classroom. Tim and Emma avoid each other all day. Neither of them know what to say to the other.

After classes let out, the children gleefully continue to pass out candy and heart-shaped cards in the front of the school. Tim, who does not have a traditional card or piece of candy for Emma, runs up to her outside the building.

"Greetin's," he says in a shaky voice, "Are you going to have a walk home?"

Emma smiles shyly and nods.

"I'll walk you if you'd like?" He extends his hand and Emma takes it. They avoid eye contact as they leave the school grounds. Emma, happy to be holding Tim's hand, cannot help but notice other girls, especially the older ones, getting flowers from their valentines, but Tim has nothing with him except his schoolbooks.

***

The Washington spring weather is so perfectly quiet, it seems as if it is not there. Trees stand gracefully in yards amidst grass looking as soft as fur in the sunshine. The pair walk all the way to Emma's house without a word.

Emma abruptly unclasps her hand from Tim's, struts to her front door, turns to say, "Thank you," and goes inside. Tim, although proud to have Emma as his valentine, winces slightly. He walks home and processes the whole day over and over. *Perchance I'm not appealin' to her,* he asks himself.

That night Emma lies in bed while the crescent moon casts grey light through her open window. Without the sun, her soft pink blankets have a purplish tint. Her thick quilt cloaks her body in warmth while a cool breeze flows from the window and across her face. Her eyes grow heavy as her delicate body begins to melt into the mattress. Suddenly, the sound of a clear *tink* on her window startles her. Emma remains in bed, but a second *tink* stirs her out from under her sheets to see what caused the noise.

"Emma!" Tim whispers loudly from the ground outside, holding a few pebbles. "Are you awake?"

"Tim?"

"Come down, I have something to show you!" he whispers.

"What? No! I am going back to bed. I will wake up my parents if I go downstairs."

"Don't go down the stairs, just leap! I'll catch you!" Tim says jokingly.

"Wha… you… you're such a batty boy! I am not going to jump!"

Tim laughs. "I am just sawin' with ya! Come on and climb down on the side. I really have got a thing to show you."

Slightly frustrated, but curious, Emma grabs a coat and some thick leather boots. She climbs down and they take off down the street, guided by the moonlight, covered by the dark, and fueled with youth. Tim holds Emma's hand the entire time. They venture down streets she doesn't know, until they come to a cemetery.

"Come on," Tim whispers, "but be quiet. We are not supposed to be in a cemetery at night." Emma's fear compels her to grab Tim's arm. His eyes light up when he feels her so close. Their path takes them past headstones covered with vines. An owl hoots, just to let them know she is there. Clouds cover the stars, leaving the moon lonely in the sky. Tim props the jacket of his collar up as the brisk wind blows their frosty breath away.

As the two approach the back of the cemetery, Emma hears Tim say, "We're here," in a hushed tone.

"I can't see anything," she says.

"Look at the tree, you see the carvin' there?"

"I can see something, but I don't know what it is; it's too dark."

"Here, let me help you," Tim lifts her hand and traces her fingers in the carved indentions on the tree

—a rounded heart with writing in the middle of it. Her fingertips grow cold against the coarse bark of the trunk.

"I carved my name into a tree. I put an 'and' under it… now you put your name." Tim pulls out a pocketknife and hands it to her.

"What would I do that for?" Emma asks.

Tim's face falls, but he continues, guarded by the blackness of the night. "Because my mother said she and my father did it when they were young, and I just wanted to do it, too, but with you."

"Oh, I see, carving our names into a tree. Oughtn't it to be a heart though?"

"It is a heart!" Tim says. "It's hard to carve on a tree, that's all. The temperature makes the bark harder. It came out a little round. I promise I'm good with my hands. No one else would have been able to do it better."

Emma smiles at his sensitivity and takes the knife from him. "You know, you are quite a funny boy, Timmy." Then she carves her name into the tree. Tim smiles in the dark but doesn't respond; he isn't sure if being called "funny" is good or bad. When Emma returns the knife, he sits down and fiddles with the blade a bit.

"You like it?" he asks. "My daddy gave it to me. It was his as a boy."

"It's a nice knife, Tim," Emma answers and sits beside him, not sure what else to say.

The rustling trees and creaking crickets add melody to the whistling air. The ground is chilly and hard, and the darkness is unsettling, but that's not enough to quash the pleasure of being alone together.

"Hey," Emma asks to interrupt the silence, "have you got any brothers or sisters?"

"Nope. Just me. My parents couldn't have anymore. What about you?"

"No," Emma responds. "What do you mean they couldn't have anymore?"

"My father went away when I was little. Mother said he blessed her with me and then left."

"Oh, I'm sorry. Did he go far?"

"No, he is right there, next to my grandpa." Tim points to a pair of gravestones. Emma gulps. After a moment of silence, she mentions how late it is getting. Tim, realizing he has lost track of time, stands up. "Well, I guess we gotta get git!"

"'Gotta get git?'" Emma repeats the foreign phrase.

"Yes, have you never heard of that before?"

Emma rubs her arms for warmth and shakes her head.

"It just means we gotta get somewhere, usually to go home. Mother always says it to me," Tim explains.

"Oh, very well... then let's get git!" Emma repeats with a smile. Tim laughs and they walk back to her house together.

When they return, Tim lifts her up against the wall while she climbs up to her room. She notices how strong he is.

"I will see you tomorrow in school!" Tim whispers loudly and takes off down the street.

"Bye!" Emma watches him go and then crawls into bed. She falls asleep saying her usual bedtime prayer, however, this time she adds a blessing for Tim. She closes her eyes and falls asleep with a smile on her face.

"THIS IS MY HOUSE!" Emma hears her father shout from her parents' bedroom downstairs. A loud thud vibrates the house as her father punches a wall. Emma grips her blanket tightly and lifts it over her face. Two more thuds follow but they eventually stop, assuredly because her father's hand has grown sore. She hears her mother cry. Her father's bare feet stomp into the kitchen. A soft light glows under Emma's bedroom door. Cabinet doors slap against one another as her father aggressively flings them open. The sound of shattering glass causes Emma to pull her blanket over her head farther. Her mother's cries now come from the kitchen, but they are quickly drowned out as her father rages on.

Emma can't hold back her tears. Her fear slowly fades as the noises from downstairs subside. The light under her door goes black. Emma waits a minute before crawling out from under her blanket. Stepping lightly across the floor, she cracks open her door. Peering down the stairs, she sees her mother lying on the couch with a throw blanket draped over her. Emma shuts her door and begins to run back to her bed. Suddenly, she stops and turns around. She runs back to her door, locks it, and then jumps into her bed.

***

The following morning Emma sits in front of Tim in class, as she will always do now. He taps her on the shoulder and whispers, "Take this." She reaches under the desk expecting to find a folded sheet of paper, but instead takes a thin rough leaf from his hand. She notices how green it is, and that there is a thick coating of red Crayola on the back. She flips it over and to her surprise, finds a poem.

I got this from our carved tree,
To show how much you mean to me.
I made it your favorite color, red.
I think you are pretty. You are my best friend.
From Tim

***

Emma soars back to reality as her son runs up the stairs to find her.

"Mommy! Mommy! Are you here?"

After gingerly setting the leaf back in the jewelry box, Emma gets up and comes out of the wardrobe.

"Yes, Leo, I am here. I was packing my closet."

"Oh, I can help! I moved my toys like you asked!"

"Yes, dear, you can start taking the clothes at the top of the stairs down to Grandma."

"Oh, boy!" Leo sprints out of the room.

When did he get so big? I can't believe he is starting school in just a few weeks, Emma ponders with a smile and a sigh.

"Emma dear, are you up there?" her mother shouts from the bottom of the stairs.

"Yes, what it is it?" She hears her mother's footsteps on the stairwell. As the elderly lady enters the room, Emma asks, "Are you well?"

Mrs. Wexford does not respond. She stares at Emma for a moment and then walks about, touching the walls and examining the floor.

"Almost finished, it appears," she says.

"Yes, ma'am." Emma opens her wardrobe doors again and unhooks a canary yellow vest, folding it in the air.

"Emma."

"Mhm?"

"Emma, I'm familiar with the look in your eye. You know that wise woman would want you to be happy."

Emma spins around and looks down at the floor. "I am aware."

Mrs. Wexford brushes her daughter's bangs from her forehead and then kisses the top of her head. "I am going to prepare tea if you would care for any?"

"Yes, I'll finish here and then join you."

Mrs. Wexford smiles and then leaves. Emma waits for her footsteps to reach the bottom of the stairs, then enters her closet again and sits by the jewelry box. She picks it up and in a hushed tone, murmurs her son's name, "Leo," as her mind travels back in time once more.

***

"Cheers, cheers, cheers!" Her classmates sing

and clap as the teacher announces that Emma is turning sixteen. She is a little embarrassed at being the center of attention, but Tim is right behind her and she always feels comfort beside him. He now has broad shoulders and thick, curly brown hair. His voice has deepened and his soft skin has been replaced with a light layer of stubble that gradually takes over his cheeks. Emma is maturing into a young lady. Her eyes have softened, her skin glows, and her posture is proudly upright.

"You're not fond of having the first day of class coincide with your birthday, huh?" Tim needles her.

Emma twists around and concedes, "I am alright with it. I am just quite amazed at how fast our summer went by this year."

Charlie, sitting behind Tim, butts into the conversation. "As always, you and Tim were together all summer... again. I didn't even get to see my best friend!" Tim puts his hand on Charlie's face and pushes him back into his seat.

"I am sorry, Charlie!" Emma apologizes sincerely.

"You're fine, Emma. I spent time with Charlie plenty this summer," Tim says.

Emma thinks back to the summer, to the summers before, and to all her memories with Tim. She replays their time together and sees how their relationship grew every day as simply as turning the pages of a book. Her eyes flutter with each memory— one in particular from when she and Tim had known each other for only a year. It was an autumn night and her father and mother were arguing intensely late into the evening. Emma heard a loud shout and the sound of a wooden chair-leg snapping in the kitchen. She sneaked out of her house, running to Tim's with tears streaming down her face. He let her into his room through his window without asking any questions and gave up his bed for her, making a pallet for himself on the floor. In the middle of the night Emma moved down to the floor with him and he held her as she cried herself to sleep. In the morning the sun shone on Emma with a new light, as she forgot the pain of the night before, only knowing how warm and safe her heart felt with Tim.

The school bell rings the end of another day of classes, and Tim takes Emma's hand to walk her home, as he always does now. On the way home, she asks, "Did you have fun being with me this summer? I know you missed a lot of your other friends when you were with me."

Tim brings her hand up to his face and gives it a soft kiss. "Between you and me, I had much rather been with you."

Emma blushes. She is incapable of hiding her happiness. "I hope every summer will be like this past one. Before I moved here, I stayed home all day."

"That doesn't seem like fun at all. I wouldn't want my kid to stay at home all day over the summer; that would make me sad, too," Tim responds.

"Well, perhaps I wasn't familiar with anything different."

Tim laughs. "If I were your dad, I would have

said, 'Emmeline, go outside and have some fun' or something!"

Now Emma is laughing, too.

"Do your parents usually call you Emmeline or Emma? I can't remember."

"Emmeline, but you want to know something?"

"What?"

"If I were to have been born a boy, my parents were going to call me Noah. Can you believe that? I don't think I look anything like a *Noah*."

Tim laughs hard. "If I happened to be a girl, my mom said she was going to have me named Tiffany Grace."

Emma smiles and teases, "Oh, Tiffany Grace! Thank you so much for walking me home. You really are a lady!"

Tim tries to scowl but is unable to stop laughing. "As it happens, I know what I am going to name my son already," he announces.

"Oh? What is it?"

"Leonidas," he says proudly.

Emma frowns. "Leonidas? Tim, you are sawing..."

"No, it is a good name. And if you would like, you could call him Lee or Leo. I would prefer Leo," he says grinning.

"So... you *are* being honest," Emma says in a disappointed tone.

"What's wrong with Leo or Lee? Isn't that one of your cousins' names?"

"Who are you talking about?"

"You know. Remember when I met your three cousins, Albert, Henri and the other one? They work at that Christmas shop… remember? You introduced them as your 'Sadacca cousins' because they are the only ones on your dad's side that don't have Wexford as their last name

"You mean *Leon*?"

"Yes, Leon Sadacca! That's the same as Leo," he says. Emma rolls her eyes and keeps walking.

Just as they turn the corner towards Emma's house, Tim stops. "What's wrong?" she asks.

"Nothing," he responds. "I simply almost forgot to give you your birthday present." Tim pulls out a folded sheet of paper.

"You know I said you didn't have to do anything for me!"

"Read it. I wrote it for you," he says. Emma unfolds the paper and reads:

A kiss goodnight and we lie to sleep.
Eyelids close to an unconscious scene.
My feet in sand, a silent storm touches the shore.
Beauty all around, awake in a dream.

Soundless, I blend into downpour.
Rain cascades and fills the ocean with clear waves.
Lightning paints the horizon in
streaks without thunder.
A dark blue sky contoured with
clouds thick, and paved.

Cool wind on the skin and in the
lungs stirs a subtle shudder.

Perfect silence, I know can never happen again.
Goodbye beautiful storm, my eyes open anew.
I will not miss the quiet clouds and rain,
For I wake to a greater beauty in you.
From Tim

At the last words, Emma throws her arms around Tim and hugs him as hard as she can. "I love it!"

Grateful, he holds her tightly. "I was nervous about writing you another poem. I wasn't certain if you would be fond of it."

"I love all the poems you write me. This one is especially beautiful!" Emma sighs, resting her head on his chest.

As they continue to hold each other tenderly, John Calhoun and Brad Hum pass by along the other side of the street. John, upon seeing them, yells, "Hey, you two! Cut that mush out!"

Tim, right next to Emma's ear, shouts back, "After you and Brad do, Calhoun!" Emma jerks her head away. John storms across the street, with Brad right behind him.

"You think you're clever, huh, Anderson?" John snarls in Tim's face.

Tim responds, "Well, I aced the last science examination. The teacher said the class averaged a B, so perchance I might be a little clev..."

"Shut up, smart guy! You know what I meant.

What makes you think you can talk to me like that?" John barks. Brad grabs Tim's book bag and throws it on the ground.

Emma rubs her ear for a moment, then steps between John and Tim in an effort to end the quarrel. "Stop it! Tim is sorry, John. We were just on our way home."

"Whoa, don't apologize for me." Tim fixes his eyes on John.

"Yes, you owe an apology yourself!" Brad snarls.

"You can't even spell 'apology,' Hum," Tim growls back.

Brad snatches the sheet of paper from Emma's hand. "Give that back!" she yells. Brad hands it to John and blocks Tim and Emma from reaching for it. John begins to read the poem to himself. "Well, well, what's this? I wasn't familiar with your girly side, Sally Anderson!"

"John, give that back to Emma. It's hers." Tim steps in front of Emma.

"Oh, I am sorry, Emma," John says as he reaches the paper outward. "I didn't mean to be so rude! Here you are." John then rips the paper to pieces and throws it at her feet with a smirk. Tears fill her eyes as she kneels to pick up the shredded poem.

Tim's blood runs hot. He clenches his fists and swings at Brad, knocking him on the chin, and then rushes for John who jumps away, frightened.

"Don't let him hit me, Brad! I will get in trouble with my parents!" John screams.

Brad grabs Tim's shirt from behind, yanking

him to the ground, and then kicks him in the head, causing his nose to bleed. He hurls a fist towards Tim's face, but Tim rolls away just in time—Brad fractures a knuckle on the sidewalk and howls in pain. Tim gets up and punches the big brute in the face. Angry that Tim has eluded his assault thus far, Brad swings heavily at Tim's stomach. Tim leaps back avoiding the strike, and then punches Brad again, this time knocking him to the ground in a daze.

"Tim, stop it! Let's go!" Emma pleads. John, shocked at the sight of Brad defeated, takes off as fast as he can. Brad follows John across the street, stumbling in pain.

When Emma's shock subsides, she slaps Tim across the shoulder, but then her eyes begin to tear as she sees the damage to his nose. "You need to see a doctor. Are you pleased now?" Emma does not know whether to be angry or sympathetic. She looks Tim in the face while wiping her tears away.

Tim stares at the ground, refusing to look Emma directly in the eye. "I don't need a doctor. It probably looks worse than it is."

"Well... just keep your head held back. I can get you some cloths to wipe your face at my house." She takes a closer look at his nose. Angry again, she says in a sarcastic tone, "My parents are both home, so we get to enjoy their reaction at seeing you like this. Come on, now." Tim tries to breathe through his nose, but the damage has made it permanently impossible to get air through his left nostril.

As Tim holds his head back, Emma guides him

to her front porch steps, and then goes inside to get him a towel. After a few moments, she returns with her mother to nurse Tim's face. Emma's mother becomes frantic at the sight of Tim's nose, but he calms her down by assuring her that he isn't in serious pain. While her mother presses a cold, wet towel against Tim's nose, Emma walks her through the tale of what happened. Once the bleeding subsides, Mrs. Wexford invites Tim to have dinner with them, an invitation that he graciously accepts.

CHAPTER THREE

Emma folds a silk dress shirt, the last article of clothing in the wardrobe, and lays it in a leather trunk. Closing the lid, she turns to sit and rest on the suitcase, only to be blinded by beams from the setting sun coming through a window across the room. Mesmerized by its brilliance, she stands and walks toward the light. As she peers out the window, the orb's rays graze the peaks of a small spit of land out in the middle of the lake. The island grows dark under the orange glow of fading light, and Emma shudders, but does not take her gaze off the island. Stepping back, she turns and quickly crosses the room again into the wardrobe.

Her jewelry box rests on the floor. Reaching down, she picks it up carefully with both hands. Emma now backs against the wall of the closet and slides down to the floor, pulling her knees to her chest. Her eyes close as her mind travels back in time again.

***

Emma sits across from Tim—her parents each occupy one end of the dark oak table. As the fireplace crackles, a pot of thick stew sits steaming on the white tablecloth, filling the air with an ambrosial aroma. Fresh rolls nestle in a basket, wrapped up to keep warm. Smoked ham slices lay in an amber sauce on a yellow platter, arrayed with orange and green cut vegetables. A gold leaf cuff threaded with a rolled linen napkin rests on each of the four plates. Large Renaissance-style paintings of flowers adorn the walls between thick burgundy velvet drapes and gleaming wall lamps.

Flickering flames from the candles in the hanging crystal chandelier mix with the grey moonlight coming in through the windows, forming a soft glow in the room. A part-time housemaid in a heavy black gown, with a white mob hat tied below her chin, leaves the dining room, closing the door behind her—her work preparing and setting the table is done.

"I don't fancy we should get involved in Germany. All these folks who want to go fight don't know a darn thing about this country. Getting involved in other people's affairs... bunch of reubens," Mr. Wexford opines, while interrupting his statement with a sip of whiskey, or as he calls it, a "jorum of skee."

"Sometimes I am ashamed to call myself an American after listening to these things. Wilson needs to keep us minding our own business." He takes another sip.

The other three sit and eat in silence, especially Tim, who is aware that Mr. Wexford is prone to anger.

"I mean, Tim, what do you say? The boy who sold me flowers and who is now almost old enough to wear a uniform—how would you fancy being shipped off to a foreign land to die for someone else's dilemma?" Emma's father pours himself more to drink.

"Well, sir, I don't believe it is my place to have an opinion on it. I'm not old enough to fight, nor am I old enough to vote."

"Well, lad, you are an American, and you have a right to say what you want when it comes to this country, so what do you say?"

Emma can see that Tim wants to express his sentiments, but does not want to upset her father, "Daddy, I think that if the tables were turned and the Germans wanted to come here, we would like the aid of others. So, if we have men who want to go there and fight, we should let them do what their conscience dictates."

"Now, that's why I am the only one who gets to vote in this house," the old man huffs, leaning back in his chair. Then, he catches Emma giving Tim a wink, who responds with a half- smile. Mr. Wexford's eyes turn into slits as he glares at Tim.

"Let's say you *were* of proper age, Mr. Anderson. Would you take a gun over the ocean?" Wexford continues to glare as he waits for Tim's answer.

"If the president declares war, sir, I think I would take a gun," Tim replies.

"I am asking if you would go willingly for another man's dispute," Wexford presses.

Tim looks up. "I would go proudly."

Wexford stops for a moment and then leans forward. He looks Tim in the eye, "Boy, you know what I am asking you, and..."

"Robert!" Mrs. Wexford interrupts. He raises his hand in admission to his wife of his discourteousness, and then looks to Tim, waiting for a different answer.

"Yes sir, I would go willingly." Tim does not raise his eyes to meet Mr. Wexford's.

"The army could surely use him if he did," Emma adds.

"They certainly would use him, and all the other young men—more food for the lions. And what about your mother, Tim? You would go off to war and leave her behind?" Wexford finishes his glass.

Emma drops her hands into her lap and stares at her father with raised eyebrows.

"My mother raised me to challenge everything that challenges what is right, no matter how difficult it is… it wouldn't sit right with me to have another boy die where I should." Tim continues to look down at his plate.

Wexford chokes down a large bite of buttered biscuit and then erupts, "*Should*? *Should*? That's from all that propaganda! You say that as if you are required to die!" He bursts in a coughing fit.

"My mother told me not to be afraid to die. I feel I would be, though. I've thought about it, and I am terrified to die, but if I die for a proper cause then my life had purpose."

Emma smiles at Tim and spoons some stew into her mouth. Her father lowers his fist from his mouth as his cough subsides.

"Fighting for some frivolous foreigners who can't be diplomatic isn't right, my boy," Wexford continues to argue as he gets up for another drink.

"France came to our aid, Daddy..." Emma interjects.

"If the poor want to fight, then let them!" the old man hollers, and slams the whiskey bottle down on the bartop.

Silence fills the room for a few moments. Eventually murmured small talk resumes between Emma, Tim, and Mrs. Wexford as the old man pours another glass.

Toward the end of dinner, Mr. Wexford has finished his bottle and Tim has laid his silverware across his plate. Having learned the story of Tim's fight earlier that day from his wife, Emma's father asks, "Now, Tim, being the gentleman I am, I haven't moved to inquire about your face, but if you don't mind, could you tell me why your nose is swollen?"

"Sir, I wrote Emma a letter today for her birthday, and two boys from school happened to pass by. They ended up tearing Emma's note to pieces," he answers, now looking up. "I felt that she had been offended, so the boys and I quarreled, and I got hit in the face."

"A poem, Daddy! It was a beautiful poem Tim wrote me for my birthday," Emma explains.

Robert reclines back in his chair. Tim waits respectfully for him to finish chewing. He swallows and then asks, "Why do you think it would be acceptable to start a fight in front of my little girl?"

Emma cocks her head towards her father, "Daddy, it's alright. He was..."

Her father holds up his hand to silence her and continues more loudly. "I understand they tore up your little poem, but were you aware of her presence for even a moment? Did you weigh how this would upset her? Where was your self-control or your sense of responsibility? Were you even thinking at all? And you believe you are ready to go to war!"

Tim stays quiet.

Emma's mother stands up and starts clearing the table of dishes. She calls for the housemaid to assist her. Mr. Wexford continues to lecture Tim. "If you feel you are good enough for war, or good enough for my daughter, then you had better act like it."

Tim looks down and mumbles some words under his breath. Wexford's eyes narrow as he leans over the table and asks in a low tone, "What did you say?"

"I'm not," Tim repeats, loud enough for all to hear.

"What?" Emma asks.

Tim stands up, and with the same confidence he had at the door when he first spoke to Emma's father, says, "I'm not adequate for your daughter, sir. I'm not. Every day I question why Emma has had me for as long as she has because, honestly, sir, she has taught me, cared for me, helped me, and been there for me more than I could ever ask for, and I don't deserve it. I know I don't!" He is shouting, not holding anything back.

"But I love your daughter, sir. I know I can never repay her for all she has done for me. All I can give is all I have. I'm not capable of promising she will never have to worry when she is with me. I will probably give her more to worry about, but I can promise that I will always do my greatest to protect her, be there for her, and to provide for her... because I love her!"

When Tim finishes, he looks over to Emma's mother and the housemaid, who are both standing frozen in the kitchen doorway, and thanks them for the meal. He then turns to Mr. Wexford and thanks him for having him in his home. Finally, he turns to Emma, and simply nods. He excuses himself, walks to the door and leaves the house without another word.

Emma clenches her fists as her father slowly sits back in his chair. She cries, "You're not even going to speak? You're going to do no more than sit there?" A moment passes before she realizes her father has no response to give. "I wish you would trust me, Father, if only once." Emma gets up from the table and runs outside, slamming the front door behind her.

"Tim!" she shouts, chasing him down the street, the cold night air cutting through her blouse. She catches up and buries into him for a warm hug.

"What are you doing? It's freezing! Here, take my coat," Tim wraps himself around her.

"No, I'm fine. I'm sorry. My father doesn't know what to say when it comes to you. You ought not to listen to him." Emma shivers against Tim, eventually letting him put his jacket on her. After a moment in each other's arms, she leans her head back, looking him in the face. "What was it you said at dinner before you left?"

Tim smiles and rolls his eyes playfully.

"Tim, I'm sincere!" Emma says with a giggle.

"I haven't an idea as to what you're talking about, dear. I said a lot of things at dinner," he chuckles.

"Stop! You know what I mean!"

"Um, are you referring to my goopy confession?"

"I didn't find it goopy in the slightest, but yes. I want to hear it again, though. Please?"

"Why? You know I'm true to you." Tim says, playing around with her further.

"Yes, but could you just say it again for me, please?"

Not ready to stop having fun with her just yet, Tim spreads his arms wide and grins. "I adore you this much."

Emma, realizing Tim is not going to respond to her begging, decides to play along. She steps back and squints at his widespread arms, raising her eyebrows in disdain. "That's it? That's a pitiful amount. You mustn't like me at all." She playfully pushes him.

Tim laughs and grabs her for another hug. "Are you fooling me, Emma? That's all the amount of love any little kiddo in Sunday school has to offer!"

Emma bursts into laughter. "You're a funny boy, Tim. That's why I like you so much."

Tim squeezes Emma tightly and looks into her eyes. He pauses for a moment and then says, "Emma, I love you so much."

Emma smiles, "I love you, too."

Tim leans in and softly presses his lips to Emma's. She flinches slightly.

"Are you alright?" Tim asks.

"Yes, I am sorry," she replies.

"Do you trust me, Emma?"

Emma looks into Tim's golden-brown eyes for a moment, and answers, "Of course, it's just that... sometimes your confidence amazes me."

"Well, you give me the strength to be confident." He leans in to kiss her once more. This time Emma does not pull away, but instead kisses him back harder than he kisses her.

***

"Knock, knock, knock!" Emma jerks and drops the jewelry box, startled by someone at the bedroom door.

"Dear, are you in there?" Emma wipes the tears from her eyes and hurries to open the door.

"Apologies, I've been in the closet packing. Did you need me?"

Before her husband has time to respond, Leo runs up the stairs yelling, "Daddy! Daddy! Catch me!" and leaps into his father's arms. Emma smiles as her husband begins to tickle Leo, who squeals with laughter.

"You two be careful! There are a lot of fragile pieces out here," she warns as she shuts the door. Returning to the closet, she sits down and picks up the jewelry box once again. Now she pulls out the bottom drawer, her heart pounding in her chest as her vision blurs with tears. Slowly, she reaches in and then trails a thin necklace from the box.

The chain is tarnished but the gem still glitters in the light that slips through the cracks of the wardrobe doors. Emma rubs the small stone to reveal its true luster. She stares at the little benitoite pendant, remembering how it felt the first time she wore it, and then clips the chain around her neck. Her thoughts drift back to the end of the Great War, back to being young again, back to Tim.

***

"All right, class, let's get started on our presentations so we will not go over into next week. Now, who would like to read their poem first?" Ms. Walderman asks. The class does not respond. "Let's go, people. I'm aware that you are all in your last year now, and you're already thinking about moving on with your lives, but we have only a few weeks remaining and a long way to go still. If no one will volunteer, I will start picking names."

"I'll go." Tim stands up and walks to the front of the class, rattling his sheet of paper. The teacher points her pencil at him and nods.

Losing You Closely

Your eyes, oh what of your eyes,
that has not already been said,
For it seems every lavish word for eyes
has already been written and read.
Oh, what can I say about your gems
that would have any worth?
What could I say in a verse that
would have any mirth?

How to speak of such beauty
in words not yet spoke,
Still your loveliness, perpetually my feelings evoke,
So, I will write on paper what is in my heart,
Of how when you leave me, I feel split apart.

Of how your voice is so soft and so sweet,
A sound to make my heart forget to beat.
I will write of your touch always
soothing and warm,
And how my life without you would be torn.

Of how innocent you were the
night of our first kiss,
And how the day you moved away my
heart immediately began to miss.
I will write how you dazzle so,
even angels admire your glow,
Of how I love to watch the wind
dance in your hair as it flows.

I will write how the spring rain
dreams to smell like you,
And how I love your perfect hue.
I will write how your vibrant
laugh alone brightens my day,
And how for you every night I pray.

As I sit and write I find myself thinking true,
For I see now it is not your beauty

I am attracted to, but you,
So, I will write…

The class claps politely. Emma looks around the room, beaming with pride. "Well done, Tim! And quite romantic. Who is next?" Ms. Walderman asks.

Tim sets his poem on the teacher's desk and returns to his seat as another student gets up to read to the class. Emma turns around and whispers, "That was lovely!"

Tim smiles. "Thank ya."

"Aye, Anderson, don't get yourself too mushy on us before tonight," Leslie Sherman, the overzealous captain of the football team, grunts. "You've been late to practice all week for Lord knows what, you better be all brain and brawn tonight."

Tim grins and winks at Emma. "The teacher asked us to recite our poems, Sherm, calm yourself. We will still be undefeated in the morning."

"I'm just mentionin'. If you spent more time in pads instead of off writing, or who knows what, we might have been favored for tonight. Coach Baggy won't play you if you don't show your want. It's the national championship, our FIRST national championship! You cannot be flakey like ya been all week."

"I'm sorry about missing a few practices." Tim winks at Emma again. "But I told you, I fancy a win, too. I will be focused."

John Calhoun, overhearing the conversation, snickers. At the end of class, the bell rings and the students all leave the room in a heap.

CHAPTER FOUR

An orange glow casts itself across the evening sky, and then grandly recedes to welcome the moon. The football team, with pounding hearts, assembles on the grass outside the Everett high school gym in clean black long-sleeve jerseys and brown padded pants. Eighteen boys in total wait for the coach to call them onto the field for their pre-game warm-up and stretches. Some players stand and joke, laughing, while others sit and rest, focusing their minds.

Emma waits with the team. She sits next to Tim against a wall and rests her head on his shoulder while he reads out loud from her chemistry notes to prepare them both for an exam the next week.

"Water is the universal solvent with a neutral pH level. It corrodes metals, especially iron and steel," Tim reads. "Salt water and other acids expedite the corrosion. Aluminum oxide protects from..."

"I was fond of your poem today," Emma says, interrupting him.

"Well, thank you."

"What was it about?" she asks. A scuffed football rests between their legs.

"A simple story; it wasn't real."

"I'm aware, I was only wondering what its meaning was."

"Oh, well, I suppose it is about a lad who has been through a lot with someone he loves," Tim says, looking away, "and he begins to try to write of how attractive he finds her, but by the end of his writing he discovers that yes, she is a pretty one, but his true fancy is for who she is on the inside. As in... his fancy is for more than what can be seen?"

Emma laces her fingers through Tim's and looks at his hand. "How are you able to do that?"

Tim looks at her, puzzled. "Do what?"

"Just to put whatever is in your imagination, whatever you are feeling, down on paper," she explains.

Tim leans back, closes his eyes and shrugs. "I love to write, I suppose."

"Well, it's sweet." She smiles and rests her head on his arm.

Suddenly, Emma jumps up. "Oh, Tim! You have to keep teaching me how to throw the pigskin!" He laughs and stands up as well, picking up the football and tossing it to her underhanded. She catches it and hoists it over her shoulder with one arm.

"This way, right?"

Tim smiles and nods. "Yes, but remember to pivot your back foot, keep your elbow high, and twist with your waist."

Emma does as instructed and throws it accurately towards him. The ball spins through the air, landing squarely in his sturdy hands. "That was perfect! You've gotten a lot better!"

They continue to practice throwing and catching for a few seconds until Coach "Baggy" Bagshaw walks around the corner and waves his team to run around to the back of the field. Tim kisses Emma on the forehead. "You are coming over tonight still, right?"

"Of course!" Emma grins, hardly able to take her eyes off of him.

"I wish you would stay and watch, just this time. Please? It's history, I've told you, the school's first championship ever!" Tim pleads.

Emma shakes her head and kisses him on the cheek. "Watching you in that first game was enough for me. You know I can't handle seeing you get hit."

Tim rolls his eyes and smiles. With his football in hand and a dark leather helmet under his arm, he trots off to join the other players.

Emma yells a final, "Good luck!"

Tim turns to wave goodbye with his football before disappearing around the corner of the school. Emma is left alone. She picks up her yellow bag to head home. A cool tear runs down her cheek. She wipes her face and quickens her pace. As she turns the corner, she stops and wipes her face hastily. "Sarah! Hi!"

"Wexford!" Sarah March says, breaking away from her group. The two embrace with a quick hug before Sarah says, "You need to come sit with me. Tim is playing, it is the last game of our senior year and it's the dang championship! You're coming!"

Emma smiles, her eyes still damp, and shakes her head. She hoists her bag higher on her shoulder, "I can't, Sarah. I have already told you."

Sarah rolls her eyes and turns away. "You know you're missing out! I'll be sure to tell you how it was in class tomorrow!"

Emma smiles again, watching Sarah rejoin her friends. She pauses a moment, but then turns and heads off.

The evening sky shines shyly with pale light. Almost halfway to her house, Emma reaches a wide street where cars seem eager to cross quickly, perhaps in a rush to attend the game. Standing on the sidewalk near a black stop sign, waiting for the Chryslers and Fords whirling by to cease, she sees one car slow down out of the corner of her eye. It aims to cross the busy street, but eases to a stop. The driver is John Calhoun. Having spotted Emma, he pulls his bright crimson convertible to the curb.

"Hey, where is Tim?" John raises his voice to be heard over the traffic. He grins as his powerful engine rumbles. Emma glances at him, and then looks forward again.

"What do you care, John?" she replies without making eye contact.

"Oh, come now, I was only asking because I am worried. I know you both always go home a pair."

"He is at the game. You know that," Emma continues to look forward. Cars keep zipping by.

"Oh, I totally forgot about that. You know I don't care for football. Well, I hope he does well," John lies, revving his engine.

Emma glances at him with a brusque half-smile. Cars pass by like trout in a roaring river. John shouts, "Have you seen my new beezer? It's fast. I just got it last week. I am the only kid in school who has one, you know."

"Yes, I have seen it. It's nice," A break in the traffic begins to emerge.

"Listen, if you're in need of a ride, it wouldn't trouble me, I have another seat," John offers.

Emma ignores him.

Finally, a gap large enough to walk through appears, and Emma steps into the road. Without warning, one car speeds up, closing the gap, forcing her back onto the sidewalk. John parks his car, gets out, and opens the passenger door, extending his hand to her. "Come now, just get in. We live in the same direction."

Emma looks at the stampede of cars continuing to roar by. "You'll take me home the moment I'm in?"

"Yes, the very moment," he assures her.

Emma reluctantly places her hand in his and climbs into the passenger seat. John, smiling with all his teeth showing, runs swiftly to the driver's seat. A small gap in the traffic appears. He accelerates quickly and gets across in plenty of time.

His motor-car is fast, Emma thinks as the wind swirls over the open vehicle and through her waving hair. John leans back with only one hand on the wheel. "So, uh, how are you?"

Emma looks out her side of the crimson car,

trying to hide her exhilaration, and responds casually, "I am fine."

As John drives down the street, Emma enjoys the rapidly shifting images of lush trees stretching shadows across lawns in the dimming light. A dog, resting in the dirt by some bushes, appears and disappears as the wind flows over Emma's skin and the scenery constantly changes.

"Are you certain of being fine? You have been awfully quiet."

"I am fine, John."

"Alright, I was just venturing. Your eyes seem irritated and red, as if you have been crying or something of the sort..." he presses.

Emma lowers her head and shuts her eyes. "I have not been crying." Her lip quivers slightly. "Hey, it's okay. It's Tim, huh? You wanted him to walk with you today," John guesses. Emma continues to look out her side of the car. "Well, don't worry. He will be back."

Emma looks up at John, confused. "Why are you being so kind to me?"

"I am a kind boy, Emma. I just have a rough side to me." John looks at her with his shiny hair and grins.

Emma continues looking at this *new* John Calhoun. He has her attention now and playfully growls, in reference to his "rough side." She is smiling, although she doesn't quite know why. *He is kind*, she thinks.

As John continues to talk, Emma notices the vivid color of his shirt and how it changes hue in the transitioning light from deep azure to a gripping blue. His pants appear fresh off the rack and pressed. His shoes are of fine leather and shiny from heel to toe. She becomes aware of the smell of the dyed alabaster leather seats and the dashboard, made of polished wood. The thick stitching seems handmade, and the windshield is so clear it looks like one could pass their hand through the glass, touching nothing but air. "Lozier" can be seen sewn in the steering wheel.

John is charming and polite. He knows how to act like a gentleman when a lady is present, and Emma takes note. Her mind gently drifts into wonder. As she continues to listen to John talk, she imagines being with someone like him, someone with money, who could always provide for her and a family without any care or worry. She leisurely thinks herself into fantasy.

John stops the car abruptly. "Oh, my goodness! Drat."

Emma shakes herself back into the present and asks, "What? Is something the matter?" She turns to look around, and her gaze widens to fit the expanse of what her mind strains to believe is real. A dreamland of beautiful homes and fountains surround her in a three-hundred-and-sixty-degree array of affluence. Cascading evening light spans across brick pathways that grace every mansion. At least two cars accompany each house and match the homes in both expense and luxury. Emma is speechless.

"I seem to have been distracted and drove to my own neighborhood," John lies again.

Emma wonders for a moment if he did it on purpose, but she is too distracted by all the beauty to care. "No, you're fine, John, I didn't notice we went the wrong way either," she says in a light voice, still gazing at the houses. "Which one is yours?"

John is just about to shift the car into drive, but pauses, pleased with her interest. "That one there is mine." He leans over her to indicate a house on the corner. His arm brushes her shoulder.

"Oh, I see," Emma says.

John lives in the tallest house on the street by far. Two giant chalk-white columns flank the façade, standing on either side of the front porch to support a balcony on the third floor. Thick grass covers the front lawn and paves the ground for ten apple trees. At the base of each tree is a five-foot circle of nutritious mulch.

Three cars—two ebony Cadillacs and one emerald Rolls-Royce Roadster, shine in John's driveway. Emma stares in disbelief that a person could live in such a place, and it is all she can do to imagine just how stunning the inside must look if she were to take a peek.

John purposely leans close to her as she peers. Emma turns and finds her face only inches from his. His cologne is delectable. She senses his right arm drape the back of her seat while the other is on her passenger car door. John then slowly lets his arm make its way to Emma's legs as he presses up closer to her. John sees that her eyes do not register a mind fully aware. She is awestruck by everything—the houses, the cars, John's clothes, his wealth. He runs his right hand through her soft blond hair and lowers his lips toward hers with closed eyes. She watches it happen. Emma crouches as far back as possible in her seat until her natural reaction to pull away cannot get her any further. She simply closes her eyes and lets his money touch her lips.

He is new to her.

Soon, her eyes flare open and she pulls her face to the side aggressively. John pulls back slightly while she looks away, panting in a panic. She looks at him again. Their eyes meet, and he leans in again to kiss her. This time she pushes him back with both hands, back into his seat. Realizing she is changing her mind, John furiously lunges after her. John is used to getting things his way. He prepares to have her again. As he rapidly comes close, she slaps him across the face, forcing him back into his seat. John is shocked. Emma grimaces with disgust. She sees John for what he truly is. Tears run down her face. She is angry at him and at herself. She props up in her seat and wipes her eyes. "Take me home, now." John, still rubbing his sore face, silently shifts gears and drives Emma home.

When they pull up to Emma's house, she gets out, slams the car door hard, and pounds her way up the porch steps. She scurries inside without a word, runs to her room and falls on her bed, burying her face into her pillow while sobbing uncontrollably. She cries and cries, heaving until her stomach grows sore. Finally, her eyelids feel heavy, so she lets them close.

Emma sits up abruptly to find that she has

napped for half an hour. She doesn't even remember falling asleep. She looks at the clock and sees that Tim's game started almost an hour ago.

She hops out of bed and runs to the living room. The sky is dark outside, and only a few lamps are lit in the house. Finding her mother knitting on the couch with the radio tuned to the reporting station for the game, Emma sits and listens.

"What's the score, Mother?"

"I am not sure. The other team I believe has yet to score, and Tim has thrown one touchdown pass," Mrs. Wexford explains.

Emma's face lights up. "Oh joy, he is winning!" She leans into the radio and folds her hands together nervously.

"Emmeline, you stepped in a little later than usual today. Is everything alright?" Mrs. Wexford asks, while minding her knitting.

"Yes, remember? I told you I was going to wait with Tim today until he started his game."

"So, that boy who dropped you off today...?"

"Oh, that was John. He just offered me a ride. You're familiar with him, Mother," Emma answers dismissively.

"And the quarterback Adam Anderson was just sacked for a loss of five," the radio buzzes.

"Tim doesn't fancy that boy, does he?" Mrs. Wexford asks.

"No, not quite. But he just gave me a ride, that's all," Emma repeats. There is a pause.

"He has a nice motor car," Mrs. Wexford comments.

"Yes, it is nice."

"And Everett High fumbles the ball. Anderson seems to be struggling now against this defense."

"You know, Emmeline, Tim has always been good to you. I won't argue that. But as your mother, I can't help but worry about your future with him. He has no goals, no ambition, and no security for you," Mrs. Wexford confesses.

"He does have goals, Mother. He is going to be a writer," Emma replies defensively.

Mrs. Wexford frowns. "A writer? What is he going to write? No, that won't do for you. If he were to get over that football business, then he might make something of himself."

Emma ignores her mother. Mrs. Wexford waits for a response, but to no avail. A few minutes pass before she plops her knitting on her knees and blurts, "Goodness, a writer! The war is over. Men can be anything they want to be in this country." She raises her hands in the air. "Do you think my mother would have even let me consider your father, had he not been as successful as he is at running his business? I am worried, Emmeline."

"Well, you oughtn't to worry. Tim promised he will always provide for us. You don't need to doubt him," Emma replies smugly.

"I don't doubt him, I simply doubt his upbringing. You know he hasn't had a father to guide him or pass on any business sense. He has had that menial job as a gardener in that rotting flower shop for as long as we can remember." Mrs. Wexford looks down and pretends to resume her knitting. "I would be surprised if he is even able to help feed his mother from that. All I am saying is that I suggest you at least look around. Like, at that fine boy John for example. He offered to take you home, didn't he? He may be looking to court you."

Emma covers her mouth to contain a gasp as the announcer shouts, "And Anderson is hurt! Everett High is up by nine, but without their quarterback it doesn't look too promising." She leans toward the radio, focused on the transmission.

There is a long silence. A minute passes with nothing but the radio buzz. Mrs. Wexford finally sets her knitting down on the table and turns toward Emma, who stands up and stares at her mother. She wants to speak, but does not; still, her eyes reveal all her feelings. Mrs. Wexford stares back, proud of her suggestion. Emma runs to her room. Plopping on her bed, she hears the radio from downstairs. "And that's it folks! We have our ballgame! Everett High is victorious! Going undefeated and winning the championship sixteen to seven!"

Emma lies in bed, thinking over the day. She has never considered being with someone other than Tim until that evening. Then she touches her lips and remembers John, and her mother's words. She wishes to talk to Sarah, but remembers the phone is downstairs in the most public room of the house. Also, Sarah is likely not back home yet from the game.

Almost an hour passes. Emma gets up and

opens a teal jewelry box on her dresser. She takes out over a dozen sheets of folded paper, climbs onto her bed and sits with her legs crossed, spreading the papers across the bed in front of her. She begins to read. It is a poem by Tim; all of them are.

> *A hidden field of gamboge wildflowers*
> *blooms this day.*
> *I pass by and smell the sweet nectars that grace the air.*
> *I stop and think of you, as pretty things*
> *often make me do, and say,*
> *"She would love this, too, so I care not*
> *for the effort in this to share."*
>
> *I ponder, why does this endeavor not induce*
> *a bother in me?*
> *The high sun shines smooth as my*
> *mind ticks to answer.*
> *Such work to bring her here, but joy supreme*
> *once her blue eyes see,*
> *Work is happy if done out of my devotion for her love.*
> *I turn to get you, dear, impatient and fast.*
> *I do because I love you, so I give my strongest run.*
> *I do not do from a request, for a man, true,*
> *Simply does out of love for his one.*
> *From Tim*

She finishes the first poem, and then moves on to another, and then another, and then another.

> *Summers with you grow me into a man.*

Your time and patience mature me in you,
From the first kiss that turned your nerves to tears,

To piggybacks when you break your gold high heels.
I hope I am enough for your love each day,
For if I'm not, I fear you should forget me.
From Tim

She continues until she has read them all, remembering the way her heart pounded when she read each one for the first time.

Emma does not sleep all night. When she finally reaches for the clock and sees it is one a.m., she gets out of bed, throws on a coat and sneaks out her window.

***

A tap on Tim's window wakes him. He hurries to open it and helps Emma inside. Throwing her arms around him, she whispers in his ear, "Congratulations! Mother and I listened on the radio."

Tim wraps his arms around her, feeling the cold of her coat, and whispers back, "Thank you. It's still such a shock to think about."

He takes her hand and leads her to the bed, helping her lie down, then lies next to her with one arm over her. Exhausted from the game, he falls asleep almost immediately. Emma lies awake for a few minutes, feeling his warmth and listening to his slow steady breathing. She burrows herself into him, slips her fingers through his and drifts off to sleep.

CHAPTER FIVE

The sunlight on Tim's face coaxes his heavy eyes open. Inhaling deeply, he remembers who is sleeping beside him, and squeezes Emma tightly. She has been awake for some time.

As her eyes scan the room, she sees little more than a bed, a nightstand with one cabinet door, and a dresser. A dark water stain remains on the beige carpet under the window from many rainy nights. Apricot wallpaper with rust red stripes, yellowing from time, shows early signs of peeling. A thin circular mirror hangs over a charcoal dresser with only a football and a yo-yo placed on top. The black dresser itself doesn't match the rest of the room.

Emma keeps letting her eyes wander until they return to the yo-yo. It is flipped on its side and looks quite worn. The walls and floor stretch and distort into a blur as the wooden toy opens inside Emma's mind. It goes up and down the length of Tim's body while he dangles it from his pinky. The half-spheres pet the air as the toy glides to the ground. Plastered on one side of the toy is a burnt sienna-and-blue Lionel logo. Emma gradually sees the yo-yo as her life. Tim plays with it, up and down, as if he was content to do that on and on as long he had it in his hand.

"Good morning, Emma."

The off-white twine of the yo-yo snaps and Emma remembers she is in Tim's bed.

"Tim," she says, "Are you awake?"

He rubs her shoulder and lets out a low groan while his eyes remain shut. "You could be a professional football player, right? As in for money? Your coach said you've the talent for it, didn't he?"

A few seconds of silence pass as Tim acquiesces to the day and leaves his state of limbo. "Perhaps; I don't believe I'm certain, though. I've never thought about it." He chuckles a little at the thought. "Why are you asking?"

"I don't know," Emma answers a little too quickly, while she plays with his fingers.

Tim prods, "Come on, Emmy. What's weighing on you?"

"Nothing, I was just wondering why you don't fancy that idea. You could be like that Jim Thorpe." She turns her face toward his with a smile.

"Yes, I suppose it is possible," he agrees.

Emma turns away again. "But you don't have a desire for that, do you… you want to write."

Tim sits up. "Why are you saying all of this?"

"I am just wondering," Emma responds without looking at him.

"I can obviously tell something is bothering you." He reaches over and gently rolls her over so that he can see her face. He looks into her stark, blue eyes; she looks up into his.

"You've never been one to keep things from me. What's the matter?" Tim asks.

Emma looks away. Silence fills the room. Tim threatens with a grin, "You tell me, or I am going to tickle it out of you."

Emma rolls her eyes and laughs uncomfortably. "Stop, Tim! You know I don't like being tickled!"

Tim proceeds to tickle her sides. Emma wiggles in a fuss and tells him to quit. He continues to tickle her. "Tell me what you want to say, and I will stop!"

Emma rolls out of the bed to get away from him. After plopping to the floor, she gets up and walks to his desk. She stands with her back to the bed.

"Emma... Emma, are you alright?" he asks hesitantly.

She begins to cry softly. Tim's stomach hurts as he can only watch and not understand. "Emma, I am sorry. I didn't mean to make you cry... Emma, please stop that, I am sorry."

As he approaches, she turns and puts her hand up. "Don't, just don't." She continues to look off into the distance of the small room.

"Emma..." he starts, but her hand rises again. She tries to hold back her tears.

"You don't see it," she utters.

There is a pause before Tim ventures to ask, "What don't I see?"

"All you do is write! You write and think that will be enough, but we won't be like this forever and you act like you don't understand that," Emma blurts out as she sniffles, with tears now spilling down her cheeks.

"Enough for what?"

"Enough for us!" she says, now looking right at him.

He continues to gaze at her with concern.

"This won't work, Tim, not for me," Emma struggles as her voice softens. "I feel like I am going to grow up without you if you don't grow up yourself."

"Is this about money?" Tim asks, trying not to raise his voice. Emma rubs her shoulders while looking anywhere but at Tim.

"It is, isn't it? God, Emma, I thought we talked about this! You said money didn't matter to you, remember? Where is all of this coming from?"

"Suppose I woke up, Tim," she says, almost under her breath. He paces away from her with his hands on the back of his head, then turns around to look at her again.

"I will always provide for you... no matter what. I love you too much to not have you provided for."

Emma rolls her eyes and flings her arms in the air. "It's like hearing the same thing over and over again! You vow you will provide, but how? Not writing! You won't make money with that, so how, Tim? School is almost at an end. We have to grow up. We have to plan."

Tim lowers his head and answers softly, "I will think of something."

"Well you ought to have been thinking all this time. Don't you understand that? I feel like you just don't care!" Emma tries to keep her voice low so as not to wake his mother down the hall.

Tim whispers loudly, "Well, what do *you* want to do, Emma? Huh?"

"I don't know, but if I was with someone else, I would not have to mind this; if I was with someone who could provide for me, someone like... like John!"

The room falls silent. Tim stares at Emma. She didn't mean it, and she knows she didn't mean it when she said it, but her fear and frustration suppress any regret, so she lets the searing words burn deep into him without dousing them with an apology. He continues to look at her and say nothing more. She tries to stare back at him with firmness, but the tears in her eyes betray her effort. Emma heads to the window. She lifts it up and climbs out. Tim doesn't try to stop her; he doesn't even watch her go.

Emma runs home in the dreary morning, her coat wadded in one hand. Tears cling to her face and slide down her cheeks, slipping and drifting to the ground behind her as she continues to run. She doesn't get far before she falls to the earth, weeping without control. Lying on the dewy grass, she tries to catch her breath.

The slow sunrise shows the horizon far off in the distance. Emma wipes her face with the back of her hand and then pushes herself upright. As she sits up, a light sensation tickles the back of her neck. She doesn't move for a moment, wondering if it was just her imagination. She reaches for the back of her neck and finds a steel strand. Her eyes widen as she traces it all the way around to the front of her throat. There, she feels the strand harden and ball into something small. Searching quickly for a clasp, she takes it off and sees a silver necklace with a small sapphire swinging at the bottom. Tears pour down her face as she clutches the priceless gift to her chest.

"This had to have cost Tim everything. He must have put this on me last night when I was sleeping. How... how could I be so selfish!" Emma gets up and runs back towards Tim's house.

When she returns, she throws open the window. She pants, trying to catch her breath, while lifting her grass-stained knee across the windowsill. Tim lies awake on his bed with one arm behind his head and the other holding a tiny picture of her on his bare chest. He looks up and sees her sore, reddened eyes as she holds the necklace out in her cupped hand. He starts to sit up but Emma jumps on him, kissing him all over. She kisses his lips, his cheeks, his forehead, and then she kisses him some more.

"I am sorry, Tim! I am so, so sorry! I love you so much! I'm completely a kook!" Emma continues to press Tim with her body and kiss him. He stops her and looks into her eyes.

"You can trust me, Emma, always." Then he places a kiss on her forehead.

Emma looks at Tim as he lays his head back down on his pillow. Her eyes water as she kisses him again slowly on the lips. "I will always trust you, always." With her head resting on Tim's chest, she hangs on tightly to the necklace.

***

Emma's eyes pop open. She has no idea how long she has been in the wardrobe. The sun is low over the horizon, so she puts on a nightgown and goes into the bathroom to wash her face for bed. Then she slips on a robe and steps down the stairs. As she enters the dining room, she notices that all of her belongings have been packed up and moved out except for some items of the silver tea set to which she had allowed her family and friends to help themselves.

"Oh Emma, dear, you have been hiding from us all day," her mother chides. "Please join us for some tea. Henri and Albert were just telling us how their interview went with the newspaper last week. Can you believe it? 'NOMA Electric Co. Shocks the Stock Market!'" Mrs. Wexford slides her hand across the air, pantomiming the front-page headline of the morning's paper.

"I'd love to, but I am getting awfully tired. Please continue on without me." Emma walks around the table and gives each of her cousins a hug. "Good night. And thank you all for helping today."

After they all wish her a restful night's sleep, she turns to go back upstairs. She senses an indescribable distance between herself and those around her. Her present surroundings seem like a dream. Not until she lies in bed does reality paw at her again.

When her husband finishes escorting everyone out of the house, he goes upstairs and gets ready for bed himself. After washing up, he joins Emma in their bed. He leans over to kiss her on the cheek and says,

"Good night, sweetheart."

Emma smiles and pauses as she looks at her wedding ring. "Good night," she whispers to herself. "You did provide for me."

Rolling over to look out the window, Emma's eyes reflect the sparkling stars in the sky. As she stares at them, she picks the thought to which she will fall asleep that night. She closes her eyes and lets her mind drift back to the year 1922, back to the most memorable moment of her life, back to Tim.

***

It is Christmas Eve in the Wexford home. A fire warms the room where family and friends fill the air with music and laughter. Candles, feathered wreaths, and crimson bows adorn the entire house while a tall spruce, draped in seasonal ornaments, watches over the festivities as it stands grandly in the corner.

"The house looks fabulous, Henri!" Emma kisses her cousin on the cheek. She wears an elegant cherry velvet dress with a chocolate belt and flat black shoes. Her blonde locks are dolled up in a bun on top of her head and her lips are lightly tinted with a Levy Tube claret shade to enhance what Tim calls her "natural glow."

"Thanks! Hopefully I get more business next year after a party like this," Henri responds with a laugh.

"I am going to go find Tim. Let me know if you need anything. I think we have more eggnog in the kitchen. I see you're getting low," Emma says over the commotion of the party, tapping his nearly empty glass. She leaves Henri and mingles through the guests searching for Tim. After ruling out the living room and the two dens, she enters the kitchen and finds him talking to her mother while helping with some dirty dishes. She sighs at how handsome he looks in his festive sage green sweater and clean khaki pants, then runs over and grabs his arm.

"Mother will take care of that, Timmy. Come out and meet people!" Emma playfully pulls him out of the kitchen.

Tim is a young man now. His frame has filled out and, although he never grew beyond average height, his body has matured. In contrast, Emma has become graceful and sweet. Her hands and nails are that of a lady, and she walks with the poise that comes from maturity.

As the night develops, Tim turns into the life of the party. He encourages a game of charades that makes the guests cry with laughter. Despite being the least sophisticated person in the room, his confidence has everyone feeling honored he is there.

Tim eventually slips away while the party progresses. After a lengthy conversation with an old acquaintance, Emma scans the living room and notices he is gone. She walks around the house looking for him, but he is nowhere to be found. She begins to ask the guests if they have seen him or if they know where he went. No one seems to know, and most are too occupied with the ongoing game of charades to give her an attentive reply.

She ends up in the kitchen, finding her mother

sipping alone from a glass of golden liquid. Emma walks over and sees a bottle of wine under the table, as well as a little glaze in her mother's eyes.

"Mother! You are not supposed to have this," she scolds.

Emma's mother laughs and answers with a slight slur, "It's fine dear, it's fine. Just sit, it's fine. Here, have a drink with your mother." Emma sits, and her mother pours her a glass.

"Does Father know you have this?"

"Just drink. You are almost a twenty-year-old woman. It's fine! No Prohibitionists as far as I can see." Mrs. Wexford hands her daughter the brimming glass.

Emma takes a sip and finds that she enjoys the taste. She and her mother talk for a few minutes about the party and before either of them realizes it, Emma has drunk two glasses. "Slow yourself, dear. You need not drink so much your first time," Mrs. Wexford warns.

"I feel fine, Mother. I don't feel dizzy or sick at all. I must have Father's stomach, huh?" Emma picks up the bottle of wine and tries unsuccessfully to read the label out loud. She holds it out to her mother. "Can you tell me what this says?"

Mrs. Wexford squints her eyes and shakes her head. "I haven't a clue, dear. All I can tell you is that starts with a C. It is a German Riesling, though, really fine."

Emma examines the bottle again.

"Speaking of the Germans, have you been made aware of all the changes they are making over there since the end of the War? Some worker's party has been replaced," her mother concentrates to enunciate clearly.

"I'm not familiar with what that is, Mother."

"It doesn't matter because it is gone now. The 'N'... 'NS'... 'S'... 'DP' or 'DPA'... what was it? Oh the 'NSDAP'... no? Something like that, has replaced it. That stands for something, dear. A man named Adolf is running it now. Your father says he is a fine man."

"What makes him a fine man?" Emma asks.

Before Mrs. Wexford answers, the back door opens, and a rush of cold air fills the room. Tim stands in the kitchen with snow on his jacket and freshly melted ice on his face.

"Tim! I have been looking for you. Where have you been all of this time?" Emma scolds with narrowed eyes and a hand on her hip. Mrs. Wexford quickly places the wine under the table and looks down as if spotting a piece of food stuck on the table-cloth.

"Come with me, Emma! I have a matter I want to show you," Tim says, breathing heavily.

"Alright, but where have you been?" Emma grabs her coat.

Mr. Wexford walks into the room. He nods at Tim, gives Emma a kiss on the top of her head, and walks down the hall towards his bedroom. Mrs. Wexford smiles seductively and follows her husband. From the kitchen, Tim and Emma hear the bedroom door shut behind Emma's mother.

"Your mom all right?" Tim asks.

"Yes, she just has the Christmas spirit. Where are we going? It is awfully cold outside."

Tim grabs Emma's hand. "Come, it isn't that bad. It is getting darker, but the wind is actually dying down."

Holding her hand firmly, he leads her outside. The crisp, natural air refreshes their faces. The falling snow has stopped, and the wind slows. They cross the yard and head down the street, huddling close together to keep warm.

"Where are you taking us? It's Christmas Eve, you know," Emma says, happily patting a foot into the snow with each step.

"I can't tell you; I have to show you," Tim answers with a nervous smile. Emma can see him shaking more than what the cold calls for.

"Are we going back to your place?" she asks.

"No, now don't ask any more, I don't want you to ruin the surprise." Emma scrunches her nose up at Tim but decides not to pry any further. He keeps quiet as they walk.

"You're being unusually silent. Is everything fine?"

"Yes, I am just thinking. Nothing is wrong."

Emma squeezes his hand. "Promise?"

"Promise."

After walking for nearly twenty minutes, they approach a set of trees. They continue through the brush, reaching a path that leads to the edge of a cliff far behind the tree line. Emma knows the woods and recognizes this path. When they step onto it, she is confused, but continues to follow Tim. At the end of the winding trail they break through the last of the trees, and the view from atop the precipice reveals itself. Emma looks out and stares with an open mouth.

The steep ledge overlooks an ocean of white-topped oaks below that extends far off to the horizon where shaded cerulean mountains decorate the distant edges of the forest. Like the fuzzy seeds of dandelions, innumerable small flakes of snow cover the earth in innocence as they slowly fall, wispy in the air against the dark sky. The rich scent of pine trees dances in the cold air as the full picture of life seems to hold still. A gust of emotions blend within Emma as she beholds all the stars sleeping peacefully up above the clouds. The wind kisses her face as it passes to lift her hair slightly off her shoulders. She feels rooted to everything, from the earth below, to the trees by her side, to the moon up high. She lifts her arms like drooping wings, as if she is about to fly in a dream, witnessing the world through the eyes of both her body and her spirit.

"Tim! Tim, look at this sight! This is amazing, just like a painting! Do you see it all? Do you?" Emma squeals, unable to tear her eyes away from the beautiful sight. She soon realizes, however, that Tim is no longer beside her. She looks back to find him digging in the snow with a tree branch.

"Remember... remember... you need to remember..." Tim whispers to himself as his eyes scan the forest.

"Tim, what are you doing?"

"Just a moment," he responds.

He gives up digging in that area, moves to another spot and digs some more. Emma watches as Tim searches with purpose and finally shouts, "Found it!"

Digging up a small caramel shoebox from the ground and brushing the damp dirt off it, Tim stands and turns to Emma. She plods over to him in the thick snow. He opens the box in front of her.

"What is that?" she asks.

"Just wait," he answers and dashes off to a tree behind him.

Emma frowns with impatience. She leans over to try to view what he is doing. She sees him turning the crank of a machine, which turns out to be a gas-powered generator.

"What on earth are you doing? What is that?"

He doesn't reply.

"Is this what you left the party for?"

"Hold on," he says. He flips a rusted switch, and all the trees around them instantly glow with thousands of lights. They are so numerous that at first it frightens Emma. Her eyes take in the most brilliant sight she has ever seen. An overwhelming sensation of amazement and peace fills her heart as her mouth and eyes widen. Tim covers the generator with a thick wool blanket to muffle the sound of the motor. He joins Emma and opens the box again, reaching in and pulling out a sheet of paper.

"Tim, this is heavenly. How did you do this? What is all of this?" Emma asks as she marvels with her head tilted back. She looks down at Tim, who is now kneeling before her with sweat dripping down his face. "Darling, are you alright?"

Tim looks up at her, smiling. "I am fine. I want to read this to you."

Emma kneels beside him. "Of course. Go ahead."

"No, you stand up." Tim takes her hand and helps to lift her up. She hears him mutter to himself, "Alright... alright..."

Tim takes off his gloves. When he does, Emma notices his hands are shaking. He looks at her and smiles, then looks down at the sheet of paper and begins to read.

Dear Emma,
I cannot wait until the day I get to read this to you. I am writing this note now at sixteen, here on this cliff, thinking of how astounding the stars look tonight, and hoping they will look just as unbelievable when I kneel in front of you and read the poem I am about to write.
From Tim

Emma's eyes widen as she begins to understand what Tim is doing. He pulls out a second sheet of paper from the box, unfolds it, grabs her hand, and reads aloud again.

Life with you, a life devoted in love, is what I long for.
To share myself, accord my heart with
yours, I want nothing more.

Though your existence given alone
is an open blessing,
To live always with you is vivacity
too vast to voice in script.

When I see you, my vulnerable heart
dives deep into bliss,
Into paradise, a blue sea perfect and exciting.
I cherish when you take my breath
away with a touch and kiss,
For you are my ultimate jewel, fabulous
wonder, and my festive pride.

I hope with my prayers I have earned
you, at least in your eye,
For you are a treasure to me, one I vow never to hide.
I wish to wake every morning and have
your beauty be the first I see.
I love you Emmeline Lorraine Wexford.
Will you marry me?

Emma's eyes begin to water and she smiles. Then she looks into Tim's eyes through streaming tears and shouts, "Yes!" before she tackles him into the snow, kissing him like she has never kissed him before. Tim laughs jubilantly at her reaction. Emma doesn't care about anything else happening in the distant world—she is going to marry Tim. Leaning over him on the ground, she throws her head back, laughing giddily and then falls slowly over on her back. Tim lies beside her in the snow and watches her stare up at the lights, soaking in the moment. Suddenly, she turns to him with a mischievous grin, grabs a ball of snow and pies him in the face. She laughs and gets up to run away.

Tim yells, "I'm getting you for that!"

Emma screams back, "Not if you can't catch me!"

He chases her through the trees. They laugh while trying not to trip in the snow. They show their youth... they show themselves.

Emma picks up a cold ball of white, pivots her foot, raises her elbow, twists her hips, and shoots it through the air, hitting Tim square in the face with the wet slush. He stops in his tracks from the shock, and she covers her face with her hands, peeping with one eye through her fingers. He wipes his face, squints his eyes and tries not to laugh. Tim then charges at her. Playfully, he tackles her to the ground as she giggles all the way down. He starts tickling her as she laughs and screams in protest. He eventually stops, and they both lie on their backs, panting.

"Timmy, how did you make those lights?"

He grins. "I paid attention in science class, I suppose. It's like that circuit we made, only with more resistors. I made them for you."

"They are amazing. Like little fairies or spirits glowing in the leaves. My cousin Henri would love to see these. They make Christmas Eve look so special." They lay for a moment in sweet silence. Finally, Emma asks, "What do you call them?"

"I don't know, they are just lights. Do you want

to give them a name?"

Emma pauses, and then she says, "Christmas lights."

He laughs. "I fancy that. 'Christmas lights' they are. A million-dollar idea."

Emma rolls over in the snow and kisses Tim again. "Everything is just so perfect. Thank you."

He kisses her on the forehead. "You would probably want to lie here forever, but we actually should get git before we both get sick."

She kisses him once more on the lips and stands up. Tim gets up as well and brushes the snow off his jacket. He takes her hand as they begin to walk together.

"Were my parents privy to your plan for tonight?"

"Yes, I talked to them a week ago."

"Did you mention a wedding?" Emma inquires again.

"A little. I figured I would let you and your mother handle that... I've actually been working on the honeymoon trip." Tim squeezes her hand and grins.

"A trip? Where to?" Emma asks, barely able to control her excitement.

"Well, we can go over the details together, but I was thinking we travel across Europe. Starting in Germany and ending in Italy or somewhere down south."

Emma screams again and throws her arms around him once more. "You saved up for this, didn't you?"

Tim takes both her hands and looks into her glowing eyes, "You're worth it."

Together they walk over to the generator and Tim shuts it off, turning the night dark again. Emma lays her head on his shoulder as they walk back home. She stares up at the stars and whispers, "Thank you."

***

Emma rolls under the covers to the edge of the bed. Her husband is sound asleep as her memory of years ago fades into the twilight of her mind. Staring at the ceiling, her eyes soften as she recalls Tim's sweet proposal. The bed is warm, and the blankets are clean and velvety. Emma turns her head to the side. As her eyes shut for the last time, she drifts into a deep sleep, and begins to dream.

CHAPTER SIX

"I can't believe we are here in Germany!" Sitting cross-legged on the bed, Emma peers through the porthole as the first sightings of Deutschland creep over the horizon.

Tim walks over to have a look while struggling to put on a coral and navy bowtie. He takes a deep breath and exhales happily. "Finally, we can get off this boat!"

"You've never been very fond of the water. I still need to teach you how to swim better." Emma rolls her eyes. Tim opens his travel bag and begins to pack his belongings.

"I can swim fine, as long as the water is not so deep that I can't touch the bottom with my feet."

"That doesn't count!" she giggles.

The young bride opens the round window and feels the cool May breeze course through her hair and across her face. Waves splash against the large boat as it heaves toward the blinding sun high in the sky. Emma sticks her head out and looks down in time to glimpse a pair of finned shadows swimming just beneath the surface of the water. Looking up, she sees roustabouts untying ropes on the side. The boat is about to dock.

As the ship approaches the harbor, eager tourists gather on the deck, luggage in hand. Jutting out from the rocky shore to the right, a weather-beaten lighthouse roots itself in a small spit of land. Its firelight sits cold and perched in a rusted iron cage. Folkloric homes built of wood and stone pattern the coastline. Farther away, a few gothic churches act as ethereal pillars for the clouds. Townspeople with small shops await the arriving tourists as fishermen scurry to sell their catches for the day.

On the deck, Tim looks around. He notices how the clouds angle in rows towards the mainland. Each one seems to be inhaled behind the homes and churches, as if the land itself were sucking the sky away. The white vapors ultimately narrow into points and disappear beyond the horizon behind the city.   Fellow passengers loudly murmur over the view, admiring the sight, but to Tim there is something more, like the land has a mystery it begs to tell. An eerie chill creeps over him, tapping him on the back, and he turns swiftly. Behind him there is nothing. He sees only the edge of the boat and the vastness of the ocean stretched long to where the waters merge with the sky. Tim ponders a moment before he shrugs his shoulders and turns to rejoin the crowd.

The ship reaches the dock as roustabouts throw their ropes. The passengers, loaded with their belongings, make their way down the ramp, some meeting friends and loved ones, others venturing out with maps and brochures about the city. Tim and Emma stride onto the land. They look up and see a sign that reads in German, "Welcome to the Town of Emden."

Beside herself with excitement, Emma asks, "So where are we going first?"

"Well, we need to start with our living arrangements." Tim pulls out a note pad and searches for the page he needs. "Let me see... our hotel is in Constantia." The newlyweds look around and read all the surrounding signs. They are all, unfortunately, written in German. Tim looks at Emma and smiles. "Let the adventure begin!" She laughs and takes his arm as they embark down the cobblestone street, asking for directions out of a little orange translation book.

Tim insists they take a cab, but Emma wants to soak in the experience slowly, so, three hours and two carriage-rides later, they arrive at their modest hostel. Tim unties their luggage from the cart in the dreary night. Only a few glowing windows and lamps light the town. As he finishes taking off the luggage, he sees two German officials shouting and pushing a man and his daughter in front of their hostel. Although the conversation is in a foreign tongue, Tim can see that it is a serious confrontation. He grimaces at the sight of two officials yelling and behaving in such a manner in front of the little girl, and he opens his mouth.

Emma's jaw drops as she hears her husband yell, "Acting pretty tough after Versailles."

She immediately apologizes to the guards, yelling, "Bedauern! Bedauern!"

"What does that mean?" Tim asks.

She whispers, "It means 'sorry.' Now let's get inside before they come over here. How could you say that?"

It is too late. The soldiers have already decided to leave the man and his daughter alone and instead take an interest in Tim.

One of the soldiers orders the daughter and her father to remain where they are, then the two turn and approach Tim. Each step they take with their boots produces a loud thud. Both are in their late twenties and clean-shaven. The louder of the two, the one who stares at Emma and Tim as if he understood what was said, has the Star of David pinned to his chest pocket. It dangles loose, with deep carvings and scratches all over it. As this soldier approaches them, Tim takes note of the man's unkempt teeth that appear so jagged they could cut iron.

"I am sorry but please understand that you were in front of a young girl. That was not right. I did not mean to offend you," Tim explains.

The soldiers pause and examine Emma and Tim. Then they look at each other and exchange small grins before the soldier with bad teeth and the Star of David asks, "You are American, no?"

Emma stands nervously behind Tim. "Yes, we are," he states respectfully. He looks up and sees Germany's red, black, and gold pride strapped to a flagpole. Various people stroll by, carrying on with their lives, paying no attention to tourists.

"You have paper?" the soldier asks.

"Paper?"

"Yes, yes, paper. Do you have you papers?"

"Oh yes, sir." Tim pulls out his traveling documents.

The soldier takes them and shuffles through them slowly. He then asks to see Emma's papers, which she hands over as well.

The soldier looks up. "This you wife?"

Tim nods. The other soldier winks at Emma as he swirls tobacco in his right cheek.

The inquisitive soldier continues, "You are Jew I think..."

"Oh, no. I am not Jewish," Tim replies.

"Neither am I," Emma adds. Sweat builds on her forehead as the night grows darker. She looks to see if Tim's pocket watch is visible, so that she might know how long they have been held up.

"It says here..." the soldier continues in a thick accent, pointing to Tim's heritage document.

Tim looks and says, "Well, yes, my grandmother was Jewish, but I don't consider myself Jewish."

The soldier responds, "You are by law to tell me if you are Jew..."

Tim stares back, "There is no such law as that."

"It is uh... *understood* law."

"Oh," Tim says. "I'm sorry... I didn't know."

The soldier hands Tim and Emma their papers. "My name is Kaspar. I am Nazi here, see?" The man with the damaged Star of David pin points to a red, white, and black X patch on his left arm. He then points to an identical patch on his fellow soldier's arm. "You Americans I think are no good." Kaspar stares at Tim.

Emma, who is still behind Tim, remains silent but begins to shake. There is a long pause while Kaspar stands in front of Tim. Then he chuckles a bit and turns to his comrade, speaking a few words in German. Stepping closer to Tim, Kaspar whispers, "Ich werde dir die Hölle zeigan, Amerikanisch." A smile creeps across his face before he turns his back on them.

Tim exhales a sigh of relief, and Emma's hand unclenches his arm as they turn to get their luggage. Kaspar seems to show no further interest in the couple. He walks back to the other soldier and whispers something. The accompanying officer's body language grows unsettling before he reacts to Kaspar in German. "No, we can't! Are you crazy? They are American! German Jews only, those are our orders."

Tim and Emma can make out only a few of the words from the distressed soldier, but their relief is short-lived. Suddenly Tim sees the butt of Kaspar's rifle as it strikes him on the forehead. He falls to the ground. Dazed, he fades in and out of consciousness while hearing muffled noises. Kaspar's action shocks the accompanying soldier, but he spits out his tobacco and frantically follows along. He grabs Tim, whose eyes close on the image of Emma screaming in the night within Kaspar's firm grasp.

***

After an unknown amount of time, Tim struggles to open his eyes; they are puffy and red. A throbbing pulse streams through his head as his vision begins to clear. His left cheek rests on cold metal ground and his right arm is numb, having the blood flow cut off for so long. His lungs labor to inhale air thick with mildew. He looks around trying to discern his whereabouts in the dark. He senses other warm bodies around him. After managing to push himself up, Tim sit with his back against a wall. A low hum rings in his ears.

After a few minutes, his eyes get used to the darkness. With the help of faint light seeping through cracks in the ceiling, Tim can see other men in the room. Some stand, some prop themselves against the wall next to him, and others lie motionless on the floor. All are silent.

He can feel the room rocking, like it is riding on water. He hears the sound of waves sloshing against the walls, and realizes he is in the bottom of a boat. Pressing the sides of his head with both hands, Tim squeezes out a headache. In the dim moonlight, he can tell that he is wearing the same clothes, but his shoes and jacket are missing.

Tim calls, "Emma..."

Emma's voice is not heard.

"Shh! Be quiet, you. Do not make them come back down," one man whispers in a German accent.

"Who?" Tim asks.

"What do you mean 'who'?" the man snaps back.

"Who are you talking about?"

"Gott, American, I am talking about those men who threw us down here, soldiers who are taking us now!"

Tim looks at this apparently pale white man through the scattered darkness and judges him to be in his late forties. Feeling the cold steel floor with his palms, he manages to stand and wobbles over to the corner of the room where the man speaks.

"What do you mean? What is this?" Tim whispers.

"Is your memory gone or are you a fool?"

Tim stares at this stranger, trying to remember, until the man finally explains, "Hours ago we all were thrown on this boat, as one. I watched as you were dragged on. I have been for a while now listening to voices on the top deck above. I am not sure, but I suspect all down here are Jewish. Are you Jewish, American?"

"My name is Tim... and no, I am not Jewish."

"Oh, well you must be on the wrong boat... and my name is Rupert."

"You said 'they,' who are 'they'?"

"Soldiers... new soldiers."

Tim has stood up for too long. He makes his way back to the wall and slides down onto the floor again. Every swish of fluid in his head from the rocking boat nauseates him. He vomits.

He presses on the temples of his skull with tight fists and tries to recollect his memory. With eyes squeezed shut he can see Kaspar grabbing Emma. He tries to think, but only sees black, blackness so dark and thick that he feels it would eventually suffocate him the longer his mind dwells upon it. His throat is scratchy, and his neck aches.

"When you saw me, Rupert, was I alone... or was there someone else accompanying me?"

"There was your limp body only." Rupert turns back to listen to the sounds above.

Tim shuts his eyes tightly and again whispers, "Emma..." He continues to scour his mind for answers from the past few hours, but fails, and eventually falls asleep. Twenty minutes later, a wave of loud German commands from the door above startles him awake. Soldiers swarm the cellar, forcefully ordering all the captives to stand up and form a line. As they stand, the soldiers cuff them to one another, and march them to the top of the boat.

Tim stands third from the end in line. Now he begins to sweat. He is keenly aware that he does not speak the language of those around him. He follows Rupert up the stairs while soldiers yell at them from behind. When Tim's his head emerges out of the cellar doorway, he tastes crisp air for the first time in hours.

Steam rises from the captives before the wind whisks it away. The boat has docked on a large island covered by a murky fog which blocks Tim's view, but he is able to make out a large two-story brick building in the distance. Smaller brick huts tight against each other stretch like a row of teeth from the large building to the edge of the island. Other medium-sized barracks huddle sporadically inside a barbed wire fence that also extends around the entire island. Jagged rocks along a serpentine beach jut out from what can only be described as strange, carnivorous dirt. There are no trees, and no life to be seen at all. There is only the island completely surrounded by flat black water.

As Tim peers through the darkness, the horizon seems just an arm's length away. The water appears high and moves like ink. Under the somber night sky, the one familiar sight is the crescent moon; sadly, it is too far away to proffer any solace. He thinks of Emma, and fear slowly creeps under his skin and into his heart.

The captives march sluggishly through the rusty, gated fence. Guards stationed on both sides hold German Shepherds on chain leashes. Tim follows in line. He looks back and forth to see the other men linked to him all looking down. He feels his whole body shaking down to his feet. Once through the gate, the prisoners shiver as the chilly sea wind blows into their ears, blocking out commands from the German soldiers. They trudge past small huts with chipped brick walls and sinking roofs.

After crossing nearly half the island, the chained line follow into the large dimly lit building. The bricks are poor insulation, and Tim can feel the cold seeping into his bones. The captives proceed down hallways and around corners, finally shuffling through a cramped doorway into a long dim room where the soldiers command them to stop.

As his eyes become accustomed to the darkness, Tim scans the place. Hardened silt of dead skin, hair, and dirt covers the original tiles, as if the lodge had housed men for many years. Large roaches on the grimy walls flick their antennae, tasting the sweat of the new guests. Tim hears some rats scurrying i_ _ _.._ walls. The lights on the ceiling flicker as if constantly changing their minds about whether they want to stay on.

Without warning, the soldiers attack Tim and the other prisoners, beating their legs to knock them to the filthy floor. As they collapse in pain, a clean-cut man of about thirty with smooth, combed hair and a flat uniform hat tucked under his arm steps briskly through the doorway. He stops abruptly, clicking the heels of his polished boots together and stands erect and still until every eye is on him.

The officer's grey uniform wraps him tightly from neck to ankle. His narrow eyes move slowly as he surveys the new arrivals. With calculated steps, he walks along the line of men crumpled in silence on the floor. His shiny black gloves shimmer as the grimy floor squeaks with every pivot of his boots. With a stoic expression, he turns to speak to the soldiers in German. When he talks, his face and neck flush, except for the white scar stretching horizontally across his throat.

The cuffs now cause Tim's wrists to redden and burn. He stares in disbelief at what is happening around him.

Suddenly the officer bends over and grabs Tim's chin, jerking his face up, yelling at him in German.

"I don't... I..." Tim is unable to respond.

A smile spreads across the slick-haired leader's face. He crouches down to Tim's level, still holding his chin, and looks him in the eyes. "You are a very lost man, are you not? American, I am assuming?"

Tim tries to respond, "Where... are we..."

The commander chuckles and pats Tim on the shoulder. "Relax, my friend. This is your new home. I confess that I would prefer an American not to be here; it complicates things. But still, you are here now and a part of this institution. Welcome! I am Hauptleute Marcel Wolff," he says while perching agilely on the balls of his feet. "I do not feel like repeating myself in English for you, so try to catch on quickly, please. If you are confused, do as the others do."

The Hauptleute begins to stand, but crouches down again. "I will repeat one thing for you. If you decide to leave my island, you will drown. There is not land as far as your eye could see in any direction and if you try to disobey my orders, well..." He smiles. "Let me just say, we have ways to deal with that as well." Hauptleute Wolff then reaches into his pocket and takes out a glass tube capped with a tiny cork. He shows it to Tim in his open palm. Inside the tube is a whitish crystal bead.

Marcel Wolff closes his hand around the tube, stands up, and then addresses the entire room. "Ich gebe ihm drei Wochen!"

The Nazi soldiers laugh. The chained men recoil in fear, and Tim just looks around, not knowing how to react. Then he asks Marcel weakly, "Why are we here?"

Marcel states matter-of-factly, "To work."

The guards jab at the captives' ribs with their

rifle butts, ordering them to stand again. The men are prodded out of the room, walking into the nearest hallway where they are commanded to stop and stand in line. They wait as a pair of soldiers uncuff their wrists one by one and shove them through a door into another room as dingy as the last.

Inside this room, a captive is bound tightly to a table with leather straps while a man wearing a surgeon's mask leans over him under a light so bright the prisoner cannot help but squint. The surgeon lifts a metal stamp with tiny spikes forming adjustable letters and numbers from a tray filled with reddened water. He makes an adjustment to it and then punches a deep wound into the captive's bare, shaking chest and another on his forearm. The man screams as ink is rubbed into the tiny openings.

A soldier unstraps the freshly tattooed man and orders him to a corner of the room, where he is told to strip. Naked, the captive receives a bundle of ragged clothes from the soldier's hands. After donning the rags, each prisoner is pushed back into the hallway, where shackles await him. Another captive enters, and the process repeats again, until finally it is Tim's turn.

CHAPTER SEVEN

Tim's chest stings. His body shivers, his stomach grumbles, his right eyelid twitches, and his mind is fixed on his final image of Emma. Soldiers shouting orders break into his thoughts as the captives are herded into lines again with their new serial numbers and marched out of the building.

Outside, Tim sees the huts again, and how tightly packed together they are. The ones facing him press back-to-back against another set on the other side, and none have any windows. Tim is second in line as the Nazis escort them through the cold night to one of the brick huts down the row.

As Tim's line approaches its hut, he sees an en-graved "333" on the front. The Star of David has been scratched around the unit number, apparently with a rock or a knife. The door opens with a wrenching sound of metal on metal. Tim's ankles and wrists are unshackled before a soldier pushes him inside. The soldiers unchain the rest of the captives and then leave them alone in the brick cell. The light turns off when the metal door slams shut. The outside latch is closed with a loud clank.

In their new residence, having gone without

food or water for over a day, the men stumble through the darkness. Quietly with outstretched arms, they feel their way to the edges of the narrow building. Tim touches what he assumes are bookshelves embedded in the brick. The shelves line the walls all the way to the end of the hut.

He feels a hard leather bag on every shelf, and to his surprise, a warm resting body that grumbles every time he accidentally prods one of them. Once his eyes adjust to the darkness, he sees the men he entered the hut with crawling into the shelves. The bodies he felt were those of men who were already in the hut before he and the freshly stamped men came in; they had gotten first pick.

Tim finds an empty shelf at the back of the hut. He lies down uncomfortably and then whispers to himself, "This isn't for books... it's a bed."

Hearing a "shush" from above, he recognizes Rupert's voice. A wide smile crosses his face. "Rupert! Rupert, is that you?"

"American, be silent! This is not the time to talk. We must sleep like all the other men."

Upon hearing a familiar voice, the swirl of emotions brewing inside of Tim since he awoke on the boat yesterday finally exploded.

"Rupert, please, I just want to know what is happening!" Tim pleads. Rupert sighs. Carefully turning over on the tiny shelf, he looks down at his neighbor.

Rupert is distinguished-looking with a pointed jaw. His fair skin sags under large bulbous eyes. "The

Hauptleute said we are all here because we owe our country. He said we Jews are inferior, and we are supposed to make up for being Jewish by serving Germany here." His English is strong despite a thick German accent. "We will make weapons. Guns, knives, ammo, whatever we are told to make, we are to make it." Tim leans forward as he listens. "Marcel also called this place a 'prototype,' though I am not sure what he meant."

Tim whispers back, "What are we to make weapons for?"

"That I do not know, but I do know that we should do whatever they tell us to do." He scoots back into his shelf.

A quick moment in the dark passes before Tim whispers again, "It is a good thing neither you or I have much weight to us, otherwise we'd be forced to sleep on the ground tonight, huh?"

Tim hears a slight chuckle from the shelf above. "Rupert, what was that little rock Marcel showed me?"

Rupert exhales heavily. "It was a Zyklon-B pellet... toxic."

"How do you know that?"

"I am... was, a chemistry professor at a university in Munich."

Tim says nothing for a few seconds. He just stares at the bottom of Rupert's shelf, which nearly rubs his nose. "Rupert, one more thing. What did Marcel say that caused the others to laugh?"

There is a pause. "He gives you three weeks."

Tim feels a chill rush through his veins. Rupert says nothing more and goes to sleep.

As Tim lies still on his back in the darkness, he feels the wooden board stiffen his spine, and he wiggles in vain to get comfortable. He tries to place his arms under his head to add support to the hard leather sack, but the bunk is too cramped to reach both hands above his shoulders, so he settles for one arm. Suddenly the tight space begins to close in on him as his heart races and beads of sweat ooze from his pores. He tries to stretch his ankles and neck and reach for air, but with every movement the shelf seems to shrink.

Feeling like he is about to explode, he slides from the shelf and onto the floor with a thud. A puff of dirt rises around him. He inhales deeply as cool air fills the bottom of his lungs. He looks toward the ceiling, staring into pure blackness.

All of a sudden, Tim blinks as he sees a small fuchsia object flutter to the ground. He reaches for it, picks it up and sees that it is a flower petal. He looks around him on the floor and finds a multitude of identical petals scattered all about that seem to have come from nowhere.

A hazy image appears in the dark. Tim squints. As it comes into focus, he sees it is Emma holding a man's hand, his hand, by an altar. Neither of the two fictions have faces, yet the image of Tim wears a black suit and Emma, a wedding gown.

Flowers fall everywhere as the two kiss. Applause resounds in the air when the bride and groom turn to walk down the aisle of the hut. The cheers and claps sound like they come from the bricks in the walls and rise louder and louder as the images of the loving pair walk closer and closer to Tim. The noise of the cheers reaches an unbearable level, causing Tim to cover his ears tightly with his hands. The cheering mixes with the sound of heavy waters rising high into the sky. Wind lifts the bride and groom into the air like ghosts and throws them toward Tim before he raises his crossed arms over his face and screams.

The noises grow into the sound of a deafening storm, drowning out Tim's screams. The image of the couple violently dives towards him, forcing him to climb back into his shelf for cover.

***

Freezing air rushes into the barracks when the metal door flings open. It is still dark outside. A group of soldiers barge in yelling and pulling the captives from their shelves as they beat them into a single line. Tim awakes with such a jerk that his forehead bangs on the shelf above. He crawls from the wall, aching for sleep, and stands in line behind Rupert, as the soldiers cuff them to one another. Low growls come from snarling German Shepherds. Their white fangs show, and their breaths smell as if they have tasted the flesh of man before.

Tim shivers from head to toe. His back cries out in spasms. Even the satisfaction of a much needed yawn is cut short by a sharp pain in his jaw from Kaspar's blows.

With the sun still absent from the sky, the men

march outside under lanterns toward the big building. As they walk, each prisoner looks at the distant horizon, a narrow band over the thin waters. Tim now notices possibly thirty other groups of captives cuffed and walking out of neighboring huts.

The Jewish captives trudge back the way they had come just hours before, but this time they head toward a different entrance to the building. On the way, Tim notices a new, peculiar structure off in the distance, a long, closed tunnel, with hundreds of holes about five inches in diameter, punched in a row along the side. The construction is grey and massive, ten feet high, and extending over fifty yards until it is hidden by a black building. As he studies the structure, a knot grows in his gut.

Nearing the structure, the Nazis place rags over their mouths; Tim soon finds out why. Thirty yards from the tunnel, limp bodies lie piled in a large mound. Black bags contain other corpses and some of the stench, nonetheless, the overwhelming odor seeps out into the air over the island. Tim holds his breath; he almost vomits what little he has left in his stomach.

When his line enters the building in the center of the island, they follow a set of hallways which lead to what appears to be some sort of factory within the complex. The room is so large that Tim imagines it could fit the football field on which he won his national championship. He looks up to see a balcony scaling all around the upper half of the room where barred windows resemble the uppermost level of a dark and sinister church.

Incandescent lights hang dimly above massive machines with sooty arms and gears pressed against the side and back walls. Two rows of tables placed end to end divide the factory from entrance to back. Tim sees Nazis in conversation all around, especially on the balcony, but hears little over the rumble and clanking of the machines. The Nazis stop the line and unshackle Tim and his hut-mates. Then orders are given, and the captives each find a seat sit at the tables, a station by a machine, or a spot near a furnace.

Nazis who are stationed along the tables and next to the machines along the walls shout instructions. Every man has a job. Tim takes a position at the end of a manual assembly line where he attaches rifle barrels at a worktable.

As the morning progresses, the air in the bleak room grows thicker and harder to inhale while the men sweat more and more. Tim shivered when he first entered the icy confinement, but now he tugs at his shirt collar repeatedly. Furnaces roar as captives assigned to them shovel heap after heap of coal into their raging mouths. Metal banging on metal echoes off the walls, while the arms of a brass-puncher thuds every second, but the steel-mending machines shriek the loudest, not from bending steel, but from the clanking of scraps wrenched and pressing together. Those who directly feed chunks of metal into the mechanisms' bellies will eventually become partially deaf.

Metal shavings and dust float through the air. The captives dig at their dry eyes with their knuckles to ease the burn.

By late morning, a weary prisoner beside Tim starts working slower and slower until he stops completely. Tim nudges his companion. "Hey, keep working. Come now, man, keep working, don't stop." The man does not acknowledge Tim; he simply sits and stares with a blank expression. Tim keeps working, while noticing blood on the man's fingertips.

Before Tim can speak again, a Nazi approaches the prisoner and screams in his ear. The noise startles the surrounding men into working faster, but the stoic captive maintains his blank stare. Now the soldier grabs the man and throws him to the ground, bashing him with the butt of his gun and continuing to shout. Every other worker minds his work, as if they hear nothing.

The soldier beats the captive until he stops moving, then grips the battered prisoner and props him back up on his wooden stool next to Tim. The soldier nudges the man to keep working, but when the man tries to reach his hands up to obey, he falls out of his seat to the ground. The soldier commands two other prisoners to drag the fallen one out while he follows behind. As the day passes, this scene is repeated as more workers fail to maintain their labor.

Tim keeps working. After three hours of putting pieces together he notices soft yellow light blazing through the window and into the factory. He blinks a few times and wonders, *When did the sun rise?*

Tim jerks his hand as a bit of skin on his thumb is pinched while twisting a Jäger rifle together. Blood oozes out mixing the lubricating grease on his hands into the wound. Tim tries to suck the chemicals from the opening, which now burn and sting. He grasps the rifle again, grateful for the cold factory, which numbs his stiff fingers so they do not feel as much pain.

Suddenly the thought of Emma suffering the same fate flashes through his mind, and his eyes well with tears. He tries to fantasize that she somehow got back home safely, and that she has sent help to rescue him, or that all that is happening around him is the result of a dream, but the sharp pain in his hand brings him back to reality.

Tim sniffles through his one good nostril, trying not to weep. His emotions draw the attention of a soldier who quickly approaches and slaps him across the back of the head, knocking him to the ground. Tim knows the soldier's fists and rifle are coming next. The Nazi raises his gun to strike, but a surge of adrenaline rushes through Tim, and he jumps up onto his stool and begins to work. The Nazi slowly lowers his gun and laughs sadistically. Leaning over Tim's shoulder with his mouth next to Tim's ear, he says in a thick German accent, "You fear Raupe." Then he pats Tim's shoulder and walks away.

After what feels like an entire day passes, a door at the top of the balcony opens, and a worried captive enters with a wheelbarrow. He walks with effort down a flight of stairs, careful not to let the cart tip over. When he reaches the bottom step, he pulls back the blanket that rests on top of the cart and reveals that he has something of great value—bread.

A number of workers leave their machines and rush with what energy they have toward him until they hear three dozen rifles cock around them. The hungry men return to their stations and continue working while keeping their eyes on the wheelbarrow.

The man with the bread makes a circuit of the room and places a loaf by each worker. For the men sitting at gear tables, he places the loaf on the table. For the men standing and working by machines, he sets the loaf on the ground. The workers do not dare touch the food, though, not yet.

Tim's eyes grow dim as he watches the food being distributed. His dry mouth hangs open. The man with the barrel continues his route until he gets to the last long table where Tim sits. Rolling by, he pulls out a small hard loaf for each worker.

Just as he reaches Tim, a Nazi officer yells a command over the rumble of the machines. The worried man with the bread hesitates for a moment when the soldier yells, but soon goes back to handing out loaves. When he was startled, though, he accidently passed Tim without setting anything down. Tired and in pain, Tim does not notice he has been overlooked. He eventually looks down at the table and realizes he has no bread.

Tim swivels his head desperately and whispers, "*Psst, psst*! Aye... aye, you skipped me! You skipped me, come back!" The man with the wheelbarrow doesn't hear Tim's faint whisper, and peels off with the wheelbarrow.

Suddenly an officer yells, and all of the captives devour their bread like dogs in a kennel. They bite hard to tear the tough loaves apart. Many eyes water and grow red as they try to chew the dry wheat with parched mouths. Tim rubs the inside of his cheeks with his tongue as he can only sit and watch. His hand clenches his stomach to dull the pain. His mouth feels like it is packed with cotton, sucking all the moisture out of his body.

After eating for only a few seconds, the workers are commanded to go outside in groups to relieve themselves. Tim follows orders. Outside, he finds he is unable to make the ground wet. He can't find any fluid in his body, and the men who do only spray a short rusty stream into the cold air. Tim stares at the earth beneath his feet. He dry heaves heavily before puking no more than a spoonful of stomach acid.

Returning to the building, he goes straight back to work. After what feels like a lifetime, the room grows dark again with only the weak iridescent light. Over fourteen hours since they were herded into the room, the men are commanded to stop working and line up to leave. Once they are in a line, the soldiers shackle them together again and push them toward the door.

Tim looks up briefly and catches out of the corner of his eye Hauptleute Marcel walking down his line. He sees the Hauptleute stop by one captive and stare into his eyes. Marcel takes off one of his gloves and drags his bare index finger across the captive's cheek. The captive doesn't step away, but he does coil his face to the side. The Hauptleute presses hard until he finishes creating a clear streak. Then he holds his finger up to show how black and moist it has become. Marcel wipes his finger on the captive's ragged shirt before he lays his hand on the man's shoulder and speaks to him. Tim is too far away to hear what Marcel says but not too far away to see Marcel quickly grab the man's ear, jerk it toward him and begin screaming while his eyes widen like a maniac. Those captives nearest to the scene inch away as the man cries out in pain. Marcel nearly tugs the man's ear off before letting him go. The Hauptleute then smiles, puts back on his glove, and walks away.

When they exit into the night, the captives immediately gag and gasp for air as the rotten odor from the odd structure invades their nostrils. Covering their noses in vain, they walk past the pile of corpses. Tim notices that the pile is smaller than when he first saw it that morning. He also sees that some of the corpses have been moved out of the fenced area and placed into a pile by the shore.

The walk back to the hut feels shorter than the walk from it, as Tim keeps his head fixed in the direction of the corpses until they are out of view. The black bagged corpses pile by a boat dock. *The Nazis must ferry those bodies to the mainland for burial.* He lags for a moment, but the chain soon pulls him forward by the cuffs. Under the moon, Tim and the captives march with heavy feet back to their hut, back to their shelves. He agonizes over Emma, wondering where she could be, wondering how she is, wondering *if* she is.

CHAPTER EIGHT

All the men in Tim's hut lie motionless in the walls that night. Most passed out immediately; others feel their bodies dying. Some try to end their life quicker by thinking of death. Wrenching pain from hunger robs Tim of sleep as his mind swirls with thoughts of starvation, dehydration, exhaustion, stinging wounds, the stiffness of his shelf, and how much he fears what has become of Emma. He manages to slur, "Rupert... Rupert..."

"Tim?" Rupert looks down from his shelf.

Tim just breathes heavily.

Breaking the silence, a man from a shelf across the aisle begins to speak in German with irritation in his voice. Rupert responds to the man in German, and there is a brief exchange.

Cracks in the roof permit moonlight to seep into the hut. Rolling his head toward the conversation, Tim sees a glimmer bounce off the man's black face across the aisle. Despite eyelids that almost stick shut, Tim can make out that the man has only one eye. He has only a few strands of long black hair, a face that sinks in, and joints that protrude outward.

Rupert whispers to Tim, "The man over there

says we should get some rest and stop keeping the other men up. I think we should listen. He also said he can tell we have thirst, but not to worry. There will be water in the morning."

The one-eyed man speaks again, but this time in English with a slight German accent. "You must stay strong, friend. Your first days are the hardest, but your body will get used to the pain."

Tim rolls onto his back and lets out a laugh, "Comforting."

The black man recoils in offense. Then he slowly slinks his head out of his shelf. "I am not the one who put you here! You Americans always think you know better. If you keep thinking that way, you will die."

Tim snaps back, "It seems we are all going to die in here. It is only a matter of time. So why should it matter?"

The man with one eye shrugs back into his shelf, "We will all die here, but the Nazis are generous. They let us choose how we will die... through our actions."

Tim becomes agitated by this man who talks like he knows something. "If I am going to die here, then I am going to die. It doesn't matter how because at the end, it is all the same."

The one-eyed man then pulls nearly half of his body out, placing one hand on the ground, and stares at Tim, trying to peer into his soul. "No... you are wrong. Nothing could matter more. I have been here long. I have seen men die of malnutrition, disease, beaten to death, even pulled through one of the steel compactors. But those are all pleasant compared to the Raupe."

Tim's eyes shift curiously, then he too pulls slightly out of his shelf. Their conversation has gained Rupert's attention, so he sticks his head out of his shelf as well. Rupert asks, "What is the Raupe?"

The gaunt man looks up at Rupert and then down at Tim. His swollen eye focuses on Tim as he answers, "The Raupe is the tunnel structure. You see it every day to remind you it is there, silent and hungry. The Hauptleute Marcel designed it himself. Your heads alone enter in the side of it, but that is all."

The one-eyed man scrapes dirt off the floor with his fingers while he continues staring at Tim without blinking, "You can feel your body free outside, but your head remains locked in it by a metal clamp, tight around the neck with a vice."

Tim holds his breath as he continues to listen. "When your head is inside, it is as if you are suddenly blind. Even if you could try, you could not see your own hand a centimeter away from your face." The man looks up at Rupert, then back at Tim. "You can hear strong, grown men cry and squirm like children, begging to be set loose." The man pauses. "Then... you smell a bitter gas which permeates peacefully through the air and eagerly enters your lungs without asking permission."

The one-eyed man stops to take a deep gulp of air. "Then you feel it, a burning pain searing through every part of your body. It invades your whole being, and it is thorough." His bulbous eye blinks. "The pain is long, longer than you could imagine, and with each passing minute it grows."

The man's arm supporting him shakes, but he continues. "The last sounds you will hear are the human cries and screams loudly asking for something as sweet as death."

Tim and Rupert are not the only ones listening anymore. Those who understand English also pay attention now. A weak voice in the dark a few shelves down asks with a German accent, "Why is it called Raupe?"

The one-eye man turns toward the questioner, but then looks at Tim and answers as if Tim was the one who asked. "In your language it means 'caterpillar' or 'centipede,' and that is exactly what it looks like from the outside. While the men die, they flail and kick, making the whole construct seem like it has hundreds of legs."

Another voice in the room comments, "Seems fitting. We are like insects in here to the Nazis."

The one-eyed man nods and then lies back on his shelf. "Try to enjoy the pains you feel now, American, and thank God you have the strength to bear them, because the moment you cannot anymore, you belong to the Raupe." Silence fills the hut.

Tim asks, "How do you know so much about it?"

The man's eye stares at the shelf above him. "Because I entered it once. I would often place the grips of the pistols on upside-down. I knew they were tapered but it gets so dark in the factory after sunset." At this remark, Rupert sinks back into his shelf and listens intently. "I was beaten before... warned, but that one day I had gripped one too many handles improperly." The one-eyed man at this point covers the hollow crevice where his missing eye once was. "A Nazi dragged me outside into the night and shoved my head into it. The screams had already started. I guess the soldiers assumed there was not enough gas left to end my life, so they pulled me out, but not before I got to taste the air inside."

When the man talks of taste, Tim grows aware of how his tongue sticks to the roof of his mouth. "I was coughing profusely and complaining about my eyes. I remember it felt like every grain of sand on the entire coast of Germany had been sprayed under my eyelids. One of the Nazis found my squirming comical and offered to help me with the pain in my eyes... right before he pulled out a slender knife from his boot."

Tim crawls out of his shelf and over to the man. "Who enters into the Raupe? Is it only men?"

The man opens his eye and looks at Tim. "I don't understand?"

"I was with a woman before I came here, my wife. I am not familiar with where she is but is it possible they brought her here... and that *thing*?"

The man turns his face away. "Is she a Jew?"

Tim shuts his eyes tight. "They believed she was..."

The man grips Tim's shoulder, and then lies

113

back down. Tim's lips quiver as a tear runs down his face.

**

The hut door flings open abruptly and wakes the entire hut. Tim doesn't remember falling asleep on the ground. He and the others line up and stumble outside. Buckets of water wait for them. After the men guzzle down this liquid life, the previous day's regimen repeats all over again.

**

A week goes by. Tim's body gets weaker and yet stronger at the same time. His spirit, however, is diminishing. He can only think of Emma and becomes frustrated when he is unable to remember how her hair would feel or what her voice sounds like. It has only been eight days, but the long hours and lack of sleep are taking a toll on his mind. Only remnants of her remain and those are slowly fading. He thinks of giving up.

One night, Tim wakes to loud screams coming from the hut behind his. What catches his attention is that it sounds like a group of women, not men. Tim presses his ear against the wall. Finding a small crack in the bricks, he listens—the screams are shrill and frantic. The one-eyed man whispers through the darkness, "They are taken and ravished."

"Who is?"

"The women. By the Nazis."

"What women?"

"There are Jew women in all of the huts behind us."

"I've never seen women here before…"

The man explains. "It is because they go into their factory after us and into their huts before us. They don't work as long. I have only crossed their paths once since I arrived here."

As the screaming continues in the background, Tim asks, "What do they do?"

"They make uniforms and holsters." Tim's heart beats hard in response to the yells, but he calms down when the screams subside.

Rupert lies awake. He whispers to Tim, "Don't let yourself think about it. Get some rest." Tim's heart sinks as his imagination fills with what the faces of the women might look like. He sees scared daughters, sisters, and mothers, all fear-stricken in the back of a long dark hut. Darkness is all they can see, even when they look to one another for comfort. Tim notices how soft their skin is, and thus, how easily their scars must have been to carve.

The one-eyed man speaks. "You will soon learn that there is nothing you can do to stop it; then you will sleep."

Tim lies stiff on his shelf and continues to hear the pitiful cries from the women lucky enough to spend the night in their own shelves. The one-eyed man offers, "It isn't every night. Try to sleep, American."

Tim shuts his eyes.

Before Tim's mind slips away for the night, he hears a low crying through the bricks by his head. His eyes open wide. Pressing his ear against the wall, he listens again. He pays careful attention to the crying, then he whispers loudly, "Emma?" The crying stops, and a soundless pause holds still in the air.

Tim feels his heart pound in his chest as he waits for a response. From the other side of the wall, no more than a foot away, he hears his name whispered through the hole, "Tim?"

Tears stream down Tim's cheeks as he grips the wall with his fingers. "Emma!" he whispers louder. "Are you... alright?"

From the other side of the wall, through her own tears, Emma tries not to scream. "Tim!!! I've been so worried about you! Yes, I'm all right! I knew you were all right! I knew it! The women have told me how the men are treated here... I've been praying for you every night."

Tim tries to reach his finger through the hole, but he can't even squeeze halfway through. He peeks through the hole, but it is too dark to see. "Emma... Emma, I want you to promise me something. You promise me that you will do everything you can to stay alive, all right? Promise me that, and I swear to you I will get you out of here."

Emma convulses in sobs on the other side of the wall.

"Emma, has anything happened? Have... have you been touched?"

"No.' She sobs quietly now. "I've told a few of the women I am married. It is like hell when the soldiers come inside, but a few single women and widows stand in front of me when they do... some women have been taken more than once for me, it seems, but I cannot say how much longer that will last. Some women never come back at all."

Tim covers his eyes with his palms. After several moments, Emma asks, "Tim?"

"Emma, listen to me. I am going to get us out of here. For now, when soldiers come in, if one grabs you, you must cough. Try to cough so loud and hard that your stomach will come out of your mouth. Pretend to be sick when a soldier grabs you for the night. They won't fancy you if you are sick."

"What if they think I am too sick to stay in the hut? What if they find me too sick to keep alive?"

"What chance is there otherwise? Emma... please."

Emma's eyelids suddenly become heavy. She mumbles, "I... will."

Tim traces the wall with his fingers, pretending he can see her. "I will get you out of here, I promise."

Tim listens to Emma's rhythmic breathing as she sleeps. He lies back and breathes deeply as relief and gratitude flood his soul. Closing his eyes, he notices a faint, distant noise erupting from outside. Curious, he slides out of his shelf and walks to the end of the hut. Most of the men are asleep, but those who are awake whisper urgently in German for him to get back into his shelf. He continues to walk to the door. Reaching for the portal, he feels wet cloth hanging on the hinges of the door. Two captives look at each other and then back at Tim. They have wrapped their shirts around each metal hinge.

As Tim scans the steel door, a flicker of light from its center catches his eye. Bending down, he can see a tiny square hole, like the pupil of an eye, and places his own eye against it. He can see the dark building in the distance and a bonfire further away. Screams suspended in the island air travel past Tim's hut. Wind whiffs across his naked eyeball through the peephole which causes him to pull away and blink. One anonymous voice in the hut penetrates the darkness, "The Raupe."

Tim looks again at the crackling flames in the distance and tries to remember how warmth feels. Near the fire, he watches soldiers drink and harass captives while putting black bags over their heads. Thus blinded, the prisoners walk in a line against the outside wall of the tunneled complex surrounded by many soldiers, as if every Nazi in the compound has taken a break from their duties to watch Jews die. Hopelessly wailing and crying in vain for mercy, the doomed captives stand shaking, awaiting the Raupe.

All at once, soldiers aggressively rip off the black bags and shove the men's heads into the holes, laughing and jeering as the neck-clamps lock. The headless bodies kick and flail in desperation. Tim pulls his head away in horror. A few seconds later, Tim again places his eye, now blurred with tears, against the hole in time to see an officer raise and lower his hand. Once this command is given, a line of Nazis pour cobalt beads down into the building through hatches on the roof.

The Nazis quickly close the hatches to prevent

any gas from escaping. Tim stands behind the door that night for hours watching this entire event play out as captives are escorted to the Raupe, wave after wave.

When the nightmare finally ceases, soldiers pull the dead from their chambers and throw the bodies on a utility truck like sacks of sand. The truck circles the entire structure to collect all of the corpses. As the vehicle makes its way around the Raupe, Tim counts under his breath as if he is recording something.

Tim looks at the hinges of the door and grabs one of the damp shirts. He removes it from the door, which prompts the captive in the top bunk next to it to stick his head out. Tim discovers small flakes of rust beginning to form on the top hinge of the door, and picks at it. Then he wraps the shirt back around the hinge, pats the captive on the shoulder. "We will be here a long time." He takes off his own shirt and wrings it over the top hinge, adding more moisture. He then puts his shirt back on and walks to his shelf. He attempts to sleep, shivering from the cold.

CHAPTER NINE

A playful knock taps on the door of Emma's hut. Her eyes pop open in the darkness. A soldier outside the hut unlocks the door and opens it wide. More soldiers enter quietly, one by one, so as not to disturb too quickly the peace that lies within. Once inside, they all begin to shout orders. The women quickly crawl from their shelves and line up the center of the hut as best they can in response to the screams.

Emma's quarters, like Tim's, consist of tight, narrow shelves. The coarse brick wall rubbed her shoulder sore at some point during the night, which she realizes is now unbearably sensitive to the touch. She winces while she scoots out of her shelf, careful not to make contact with her shoulder. In the back of the line, Emma stands with the rest of the women.

Sniffles and wails comingle in the air. Emma shivers as she stands last in line, her hands by her side, with head bowed and eyes closed. She wobbles for a moment but catches her balance. One soldier shouts orders at the head of the hut while the other men link the women together at the wrists and ankles.

Once the soldiers fasten her wrists, the line tugs Emma forward. The women, shuffling a few inches at a time, eventually leave the hut and cross the clearing of grey land that spans between it and the black building. This line of women catches up with five others, all shackled at the wrists and ankles.

Mist seeps from the pores of the sea and mixes with the air to thicken an already dense fog. The stars and moon, incapable of driving any light through the clouds, remain invisible in the sky. Soldiers at the front lead the way with fire.

The women pause briefly, waiting for the door into the main building to open. Upon entering, they find themselves in a sizable room. Emma lifts her head. Row upon row of iron sewing wheels stretch before them with empty wicker baskets between each machine. The room appears to have been a ballroom. Smooth, compressed wooden floor-panels had probably withstood hours of dancing. Ornate chandeliers hang from an exceptionally high ceiling which overlooks a stage at the end of the room where bands must have played. Now the bare stage presents only two desks, side by side, each occupied by a woman in Nazi uniform who appear busy with paperwork.

The female captives file off into each row of sewing machines. The soldiers unshackle one line at a time and coerce the women to take seats by the automated needles. Nazi women walk in carrying baskets of fabric and set them beside each machine. Aside from a handful of soldiers who stroll up and down the rows in shiny sable boots, over three hundred women fill the room.

Each Jewish woman now reaches into her basket of fabric, pulling out a vests or a pair of jodhpurs and laces them under her machine. Soon they drop whatever they have stitched into the empty wicker basket next to them.

Emma looks around with trembling eyes as she reaches in her basket and pulls out a brown glove. She inspects it and finds that the thumb dangles by a few threads; otherwise, it looks brand new. After threading her sewing machine, she slides the glove underneath the needle and pedals her sewing wheel until the thumb is attached back onto the glove. She then drops it into the empty wicker basket. She repeats the process again, only this time she patches an olive sock.

An hour passes. Emma is suddenly aware of how chatty all the women have become. Looking around, she catches a glance from a young woman next to her. The woman looks away, but then looks back again. Her black hair dangles in thin strands from her scalp. Her eyes are brownish-yellow, like a dying leaf after transitioning from green to red in the fall. Her skin is still youthful, but only holds a soft suction to her face like that of an old woman. She smiles.

"Hallo."

Emma smiles back, "Hello."

"Oh, you speak English," the woman says.

Emma nods and then nervously turns back to her machine, sliding the cuff of a jacket under the needle.

"My mother taught me English," says the

young woman.

Emma continues to sew.

"You talk as much as my sister there..." The young woman motions toward Emma's right.

Emma turns and sees another young woman, though older than the one on her left. This woman smiles at Emma with wide open eyes.

"Oh... nice to meet you," Emma responds hesitantly. "I'm sorry. I don't feel I ought to talk much." Emma shifts her sight toward the soldiers.

"You may talk to us. The soldiers care only that their uniforms are sewn," assures the woman with patchy black hair.

Emma sees that the woman to her right still stares and smiles at her with silence.

"My name is Emma. What is your name?"

"When I said talk to *us*, I meant you may talk to *me*. Helene does not talk." Helene shakes her head in affirmation.

Emma whispers, "Why won't Helene talk?"

"I do not know. She always locked herself in her room and yelled at her husband that she was not happy. She tried to hang herself a dozen times. Her husband talked with her about it, but then one day he hung himself. Since then she has said not one word."

Emma looks at Helene. Helene turns back to her machine and continues to sew.

"I am so sorry to hear of that," Emma murmurs.

"Ya," the other woman agrees, returning to her needlework.

"You are her sister?"

The woman nods, "I am Johanna."

"It is a pleasure to meet you Johanna. My name is Emma."

"You have not been here long. You have all of your hair."

Emma runs her fingers through her hair and looks at Johanna's thinning scalp.

"If you survive long enough, that will be the first to go." Johanna watches her needle repeatedly stabbing the fabric.

"I hope we all leave before then."

"We do not leave. I have been here more than one year. Every woman stays," says Johanna.

"No, I am an American. I do not belong here. My parents, my family and friends, my country will come looking for me. They will find me and take all of us from here." Emma's voice quivers.

Johanna stops needle and eyes Emma carefully. Then she returns to sewing. "Maybe they will come for you, but not us. You are not Jewish. Nobody cares to help us."

"Yes, someone will come for all of us. My parents will get in touch with someone who will find me. Someone will find me and my husband."

Johanna stops sewing. "You have a husband here?"

"I do. He is in the hut behind ours. He and I were kidnapped," Emma says as her eyes glisten with tears.

"We are all kidnapped. Nobody has come for anyone."

Emma places her hand over her mouth and

gasps. She squeezes her eyes shut to hold back the tears.

"Have the soldiers come for you?" Johanna asks.

"What do you mean?"

"The *soldiers*..." Johanna repeats.

Emma presses her lips together and shakes her head.

"Soldiers come. They always come at night when they have no more duty," Johanna explains.

"Oh, you mean when the soldiers come into the huts at night and... take women away?"

"Yes. They take us away, back to their bunkers for the night. Often times women don't come back unless they are liked. The soldiers like shooting us when they are done. If you are liked by a soldier, though, then he keeps you for his own and tells the others to stay away from you."

"What do you mean he *keeps* you?"

"He keeps you. He won't share you with another soldier."

Emma pauses with her fabric in hand, thinking to herself, as the rest of the room rustles with spinning wheels.

"Johanna, dear... how old are you?"

"I am fourteen."

"Fourteen?" Emma shouts in a whisper. "My dear, you are a child!"

"I am the only child on the island. The soldiers do not treat me like one, though. My sister is twenty-four, but no soldier takes her. She won't talk or scream, so no man likes it with her. That is why I tell my soldier to protect us both. If he did not, Helene would most certainly be gone by now."

Emma stares at Johanna. There she sits, a child in grandmother's skin, talking to Emma of atrocities as smoothly as reciting the alphabet. Johanna doesn't look at Emma for the rest of their conversation; she simply pedals and sews.

Emma dries her eyes with a sock before sliding it under her needle.

A few moments later, Helene nudges Emma with her elbow. Emma looks over at her, but Helene only glances forward and bops her chin up. Emma frowns. "Helene, what is it?"

"Helene says that soldier keeps looking at you. I have noticed him looking at you too."

Emma continues to sew while glancing at the soldier out of the corner of her eye. He is a tall boy who leans against the bulkhead, with a long face and a protruding chin. "How is it that you say he likes me? He has yet to even smile."

"That is how these soldiers are, Emma. They do not smile, not unless they are hurting you. That is the only time I have seen my soldier smile."

When Emma turns away, the corners of the soldier's mouth curl into a half grin. Emma shivers as the Nazi continues to pierce her with his eyes.

"I wish he would not. I do not want to be liked by one of them," she says. "Johanna, can you tell your soldier to protect me, like the way he does your sister?"

"I am sorry. I could not ask that of him. This is how it is here. The new ones are always taken. You are especially pretty; it would take an army to keep one of these men from you."

Emma continues to sew, but her hands shake.

CHAPTER TEN

That evening, Emma lies in her bed as the sun sets. She knows that the men are worked longer, so Tim won't be back for at least another hour. Helene and Johanna reside in a different hut, but an older woman, one of whom Emma told she was married, always sleeps in the shelf at Emma's feet. She is the only one in the hut, other than Emma, who speaks English. She is also the reason why the other women in the hut know Emma is married.

The prisoners in Emma's hut stand around and converse or sit on the floor and play games with twigs and rocks before the sun disappears. The floor is the only alternative to the shelves and the soldiers allot the women some time to themselves before expecting them to enter their beds for the night.

The old woman who speaks English sits cross-legged on the floor by Emma's shelf. Since the shelves are too shallow for sitting, Emma stands behind her and braids her thin grey hair while periodically peering at the hole in the brick wall. The woman is old, but strong and limber for her age. Emma separates the grey strands tenderly, combing them with her fingers, occasionally reaching to catch small hairs that escape and brush against the woman's soft, tired face.

"Mausebär, are you looking through that hole again?" Her subtle voice slips through the air distinctly, like a creek trickling through the woods that has little water.

Emma quickly looks away from the wall and continues braiding. The old woman began to call Emma 'Mausebär' when the soldiers first brought Emma off the ship. She says Emma kicked and fought like a small bear, but when the soldiers locked her inside the hut she curled up as small as a mouse and wept. Although Emma has told the old woman her real name, she continues to call Emma 'Mausebär.'

"It's not that I can see what your eyes are doing, it's that you stop braiding my hair every time you look."

"I'm sorry, E." The old woman's name is Edeltraut, but she did not like the way Emma pronounced it, so she requested that Emma simply calling her 'E.'

"It is not me you should apologize to, but yourself. I told you looking through that hole would only hurt you. Occupy your mind."

"But what if something has happened to Tim?"

"If he is in any danger, then looking through that hole will not help you or him. Hope for the best, Mausebär, but never worry for the best."

"Yes, ma'am."

When Emma finishes braiding E's hair, she lays the long plait against the woman's tiny back and reaches around narrow shoulders, hugging her for a moment. She then sits down as E stands to take her place as braider.

Emma looks down the hut and studies all the women's faces. Most of them are older, although a few are younger than herself.

"There must be something we can do to escape from here. There are so many of us, and so few soldiers."

E skillfully smooths Emma's tangled golden locks without pulling any hairs. "These women have survived this island for a long time, but they do not know they are strong... the soldiers will not let them know."

"Well, I still know how strong Tim and I are," Emma declares.

"You are perhaps the only one of us whose spirit still shines." E begins to wrap the sections of fine hair with her nimble fingers.

"I will escape with Tim. It was just a misunderstanding with that soldier. Tim was brash, but how could they do this to us? You told me it's because they think I am Jewish, but the look in that one soldier's eyes... it was more than just that."

"Mausebär, I have told you how cruel the Nazis can be, how horrible the Raupe—the tight grip it has on your neck as it pumps fire inside you. You must not try to escape. Even if you do not suffer the Raupe, Tim certainly would."

"Tim and I cannot stay here, E. You cannot stay here either... none of us can."

"I have been here a long time. The only women who leave this island are those in black bags."

Light fades from the hut in layers; first tangerine light, then moonlight, then whatever reflects from the waters around the island, then nothing. Emma hears soldiers march closer and closer. They pound on the door, and the hut reverberates. The women scurry into their shelves like alley cats fleeing from a porch light.

The door swings open.

"Damen, damen, damen," one of the commanding soldiers addresses the women as four others pace the length of the hut. Two have lanterns and one has a brass flashlight. One subservient soldier with a lantern also has a sheet of paper folded in half. This soldier looks up and down the shelves before hovering his lamp over a quivering old woman. He checks his paper. "Diese frau!"

"Nein! Nein! Gott! Nein!" the old woman shouts.

The rest of the women remain motionless. Emma scoots to the back of her shelf but, in doing so, puts pressure on a weak spot in the wood which causes it to split and snap loudly, calling the attention of every ear in the hut. The soldier with the brass flashlight beams it towards Emma. "Halt!" Then he approaches her shelf.

The light in her eyes is blinding. She begins to shake. The soldier reaches for her and drags her out by her braid until she plops on the dirty floor. He feels inside her shelf and comes across the sharp splintered wood. Then he stands her up, hoisting her by her right wrist. As he raises his hand to strike her,, the one with the folded sheet of paper runs between them. The soldier with the brass flashlight shouts, "Ackerman, bewegung!"

The soldier with the paper refuses to move. He is a tall young man, perhaps a year younger than Emma. His nose is thin, as are the rest of his recognizable features, and his chin protrudes noticeably. The lantern in his left-hand warms Emma as it hangs by her. She takes a closer look and remembers him. He is the soldier who stared at her as she sewed earlier that morning.

"Ackerman...*dah*," the soldier with the flashlight concedes. He then moves to the old woman whom Ackerman had chosen moments ago from his paper. Her face drenched in tears, she kicks and cries out, but the soldiers overpower her and drag her outside with a black bag over her head. The commanding soldier at the front of the hut waits with the door open, grinning. "Beeile dich, Ackerman..."

Ackerman places one corner of the paper against Emma's cheek and traces around her chin to her other ear. "Wunderschönen"

"Ackerman!"

The commanding officer startles Ackerman and he jerks his hand back. As the lamp in his other hand swings forward, the hot glass nicks Emma's knuckles. She winces and pulls her hand to her mouth. Paying no attention to Emma's burn, Ackerman stares at her with beady sizzling eyes. He then turns abruptly and walks to face his commanding officer.

The soldiers all leave, swinging the metal door shut with a loud slam, but before he disappears, the commanding soldier says slowly, and with a chuckle, "Gute Nacht."

Tears well in Emma's eyes, and she dives into her shelf, wailing loudly. E pushes past the other women, kneels by Emma's side, and pulls Emma's burnt hand to her. She pets Emma's knuckles lightly with her fingertips in the dark room feeling for damage. Upon realizing that Emma has not been severely hurt, E begins slapping her on her thigh.

"Stupid, Mausebär, stupid! What is the matter with you? What did you do?"

"I'm sorry!" Emma sobs while trying to cover her thigh. "I didn't mean to! I don't want to be in this place anymore! I want to go home!!!"

E ceases her slapping and embraces Emma with both arms, as Emma continues to sob uncontrollably.

The door to Tim's hut slams shut with a loud thud. Seconds later, Tim's voice slips through the hole in the brick wall. "Hey, Beautiful, are you awake?"

"Tim!" Emma screams excitedly.

E releases Emma, who wipes her eyes, smearing her face with dirt.

E stares at Emma, and then walks back to her shelf to sleep.

"Fine, Emma, I am fine. Why are you crying? What's the matter?"

She wipes her nose. "It's nothing. This place is

getting the better of me."

Emma hears Tim slowly pat the wall several times. "Don't lose hope. We won't be here long, we can't be. Stay strong and keep your head low... we will get out."

Tim's last four words ring with the stubborn confidence that won her heart many years ago. Emma kisses the hole and tells him that he should sleep.

"Goodnight, Beautiful," Tim says before kissing the hole as well.

The other women in Emma's hut have long been lying in their shelves in silence. Emma closes her eyes and tries to relax. She places her hands on her stomach and breathes deeply. Eventually she lets go and sleep comes.

She sees the flame of Ackerman's lamp in her mind. The warm light casts soft shadows across his face, which exaggerates his jagged features. Johanna's words from earlier in the day play back in Emma's mind like children reciting a nursery rhyme. "He is looking at you. He is looking at you. He is looking at you."

Emma jerks awake and rolls over. She whispers, "I love you, Tim."

CHAPTER ELEVEN

A week passes, and it has taken a toll on Emma. Her hair, once the color of dandelions at the height of summer, now looks like straw. Her skin, once buoyant, now seems it would retain the imprint of a leaf if one were to fall on her. However, she still finds the strength to smile whenever she thinks of Tim.

"Mausebär, you are a quiet one. Is something the matter? Are you sick?" E asks as the sun sets outside the hut.

"No, E. Only that soldier Ackerman looked at me again today. He has looked at me for the past three days. I feel that any night now he is going to walk in here again." Emma looks at the metal door to the hut. "And I will have to do it. I know I will. I couldn't have Tim lose me, and I want him safe."

"My child, they have come before and left you here. Myself and others huddle around you too tightly and too defiantly. They are always drunk, and they always give in and take another. We will continue," E assures her.

"I am not talking for my sake... I am afraid the next time will be different."

"How can you lose your hope with such ease?

You are one of the few of us married, who knows her husband lives, yet you want to sell yourself still?"

"I don't want to sell anything, E. I do not wish to be here, I don't want to be dying, and I don't wish to spend another night lying by, witnessing another woman being taken to be ravished or taken to the Raupe!" Emma stands up angrily. "There are many things I don't want, but most of all I don't want Tim taken from me. If there is a way to protect him, any way, then there is no hesitation in my heart. Perhaps... and just perhaps, I will find great favor with Ackerman and he will let me leave. Then, I can find a way to come back and rescue you and Tim and everyone."

"Mausebär..." E embraces Emma, while Emma remains stoic with her hands by her sides. E shakes and holds back tears. Emma finally sobs into E's shoulder and wraps her arms around the old woman's hunched back. The other women take notice.

A half hour passes before irregular footsteps scuff the dirt outside the hut. Immediately, the women slide into their shelves and lie still. Howling and laughter alert them that the approaching soldiers have been drinking. The women know frenzy will ensue in a matter of seconds, but they also know they must remain in their shelves until the door opens, otherwise, the Nazis resort to violent beatings of all the women in the hut, as opposed to only taking a few and leaving.

A rowdy thud rocks the hut, as if a soldier had slipped but the metal door caught his fall. Then the lock opens with an abrupt yank. The metal screeches and the men creep inside softly to pretend they are trying not to wake the women.

Emma's tongue is dry, but she tastes the salty sweat dripping down her face. A soldier grabs a woman on a lower shelf by the arm, and then another soldier does the same to a captive on an upper shelf.

Sharp screams arise, and the hut erupts with the kicking and thrashing of limbs. A blur of torn garments and dust blinds Emma's view. A few women bunker down in the back of their shelves, but most exit their beds and rush to the back of the hut. Emma remains in her shelf while E gets up and stands by her.

The back of the hut is dense with hot, moist bodies. The smell of the unbathed women grows thicker and thicker as they press against one another to reach further back into the corners.

The soldiers shout at the women and laugh as they watch them press into a dead end. Emma holds onto E by the hem of her gown while the soldiers thrash their way through the room like a rugby scrum. Some women break away from the group and run to the other end of the hut with the door. Two soldiers pursue those women and drag them outside.

Emma feels a tug as E's dress slips from her grasp. She reaches for it, but E is lost in the crowd. Suddenly a hand grabs Emma's wrist and yanks her from her shelf with great force.

She tries to cough, but Ackerman has his hand around her throat.

"No! Stop!" Emma strains to plead amongst all

the screams and cries as her arms and legs flail in vain. "Please don't! No! No!"

One of the newer, younger soldiers stands guard at the front of the hut and opens the door when Ackerman approaches. Emma's adrenaline runs out. She now resorts to prying Ackerman's fingers from her side, but she can't get anything to budge.

Outside, Emma sees women crawling away on their hands and knees while soldiers scoff and follow. The Nazis grit their teeth while kicking dirt into the air. Ackerman, however, keeps Emma in his grasp as they step outside. He continues to carry her to the soldiers' barracks, closer to the black building.

Emma remembers Johanna's words. She can still hear the women's shouts and screams.

"Ackerman!" Emma cries. "Ackerman, put me down!"

Ackerman has carried Emma one hundred yards from her hut and has been panting for some time. He stops immediately, fatigued, but more surprised that she knows his name. He sees that she no longer puts up a fight and sets her down on her feet to catch his own breath.

Emma looks at him, brushes her ratty gown, wipes her face with one hand, first the right cheek and then the left, takes a deep breath, and then stands in front of Ackerman as casually as she can muster. Next, she sits on the ground, extends her legs straight and parallel, and lies back, shaking all over. She reaches down and grabs a handful of dirt in each hand, closing her eyes tightly.

Ackerman tilts his head in curiosity. He then smiles before stepping over Emma. With her eyes closed, she hears his belt unbuckle.

Emma sinks her front teeth into her bottom lip and turns her face to the side. Ackerman slides the back of his fingers down Emma's face lightly. He grabs the top of her gown with both hands and tears it open. Before the fabric rips any further down than her navel, she exhales greatly and grabs his wrists, pulling them up by her face.

"No... I can't. I cannot do it! Ackerman, please... please let me go!" she cries out as tears flood down her face.

At first he appears to give in to her plea. His eyes soften, and his grip loosens.

"Ah, danke," Emma sighs in relief.

Ackerman blinks three times in rapid succession, turning his soft gaze into a stern countenance once again. Then he goes back to tearing Emma's gown.

Emma screams.

A *zip* travels from her right ear to her left ear faster than a wink. Instantly, the gushing sound that accompanies splattering a watermelon onto concrete follows. Emma opens her eyes and sees one side of Ackerman's head is missing. It appears as if his cranium has exploded, leaving a gash that eliminates a portion of his skull and brain. Blood has spattered all over her face and gown and she remains petrified in place. Looking up in the distance, she sees an open window on the second floor of the central building.

Yellow light gleams from within and a silhouetted figure props a rifle on his shoulder and strolls away from the window.

Shaking, she scurries out from under Ackerman's corpse. She scoots away until she hits the outside wall of the soldiers' barracks, about six yards from the body, where she pulls her knees to her chest and buries her head, still shaking and crying. Four soldiers run over to her.

She doesn't look up, but listens as the soldiers exchange a few words before two of them lift Ackerman and carry his body away. The other two soldiers grab Emma's arms and hoist her to her feet. She is dragged back to her hut. On the way Emma makes out what little she can from the soldiers' German conversation.

"He killed Ackerman. Just like that, he kills us."

"Shut up, unless you want him to kill you too."

"Of course, I don't want him to kill me, but he is crazy."

"Exactly, which is why I said to shut up. Keep your head low around him and shut up."

The metal door slams behind her, cutting off the cold wind.

Emma folds her arms across her torn dress. She remains standing at the head of the hut. E sees her and immediately emerges from her shelf. She walks up slowly and wraps her thin arms around her tattered young friend, who begins to cry into the older woman's shoulder.

"Why do they hate us... why... why do they

have so much hate?" Emma sobs.

"Mausebär, I am sorry. I am so sorry." E brushes Emma's hair from her face. In doing so, she feels some of Ackerman's blood, but the room is so dark she cannot see its color; she assumes it must only be sweat.

"These aren't humans, these are wild, feral beasts!" Emma continues to sob.

"My child, these men are no different than the two of us. They fear, as we fear. We are here because of that and no more."

"Then why do they fear us? Why hate?"

"Because we hate what we do not understand," E squeezes Emma tightly before releasing her. The two walk back to the end of the hut. "Sleep now, Mausebär. That soldier's violation will fade in time."

Emma steps to her shelf but stops to clarify. "Oh, E, nothing happened. Ackerman was stopped, before he was able to."

"By whom?"

"I don't know... maybe by someone who understands us..."

E pauses at those words. "Sleep, Mausebär, we wake early tomorrow."

Emma slides into her shelf. She paws the hole in the wall and opens her mouth to speak but stops herself, then kisses her fingertips and presses them to the wall. Lying as close to the hole as possible, she tries to sleep.

Just as she begins to drift into a dream, someone calls her name. "Emma?"

Her eyes open and she realizes it is Tim. "Yes,

Tim!"

"My God! Are you all right? I heard the screams when I came in. E said you were gone. I almost broke my door down."

Emma rubs her heavy eyes. "Yes, I am all right. You mustn't worry, I am not hurt."

"I have been pressed against this wall without breathing, waiting to hear your voice!"

"I don't know. Please... just let me... sleep. I'm... so... tired." Her voice trails off.

"Emma, I don't understand. When were you going to tell me you were back safe? I have been worried to death..." He waits for an answer.

"Emma," he whispers one last time, then gives up and lets her sleep.

***

As the days pass, Emma returns to the black building each morning. She gets a pulse of hope from talking to Tim at night, yet the constant cold and hunger and lack of sleep have taken their toll. She sews until her blisters grow blisters. And just as Johanna said it would, her hair begins to fall from her head.

But she daydreams. She thinks of being rescued and going back home with Tim. Emma can feel the warmth of being held in his arms again. She smiles as they look into each other's eyes. Suddenly, the image is gone, and a sharp pain stings her face; a soldier has slapped her to the floor. The Nazi then grabs her hair, pulls her back up into her seat, throws a jacket into her lap and screams, "ARBIETEN!" Emma touches her face briefly and then goes back to work, straining to see as her eyes blur with tears.

By the end of day, Emma is the only woman in chains who is smiling.

Back in her hut, all of the prisoners sleep except Emma. She lies awake in her shelf, listening carefully for the men to enter their hut. It is not long after the door slams that she hears Tim whisper, "Hey, Beautiful!" through the hole in the wall. Emma exhales.

"Mmm, just hearing your voice is quite enough to keep me going, I hope you know."

Both know better than to ask about the day's drudgery.

Tim grins, "How are you managing?"

"I am fine; you have yourself to worry about, though. You shouldn't be caring for two people when it is hard enough to take care of oneself in this place."

"That is true, but on the contrary, thinking of you strengthens me. I told you we will get out of here, and I'm sincere." As Tim speaks in the darkness, he lifts his shirt. He rubs his hand down his side, noticing that his ribs visibly separate as the fingers on his hand.

Before Emma can respond, the door to her hut swings open. Icy air rushes in as she turns to see three intoxicated soldiers in the doorway. In the middle stands Kaspar with a half-empty bottle. Emma quickly rolls as far from the edge of her shelf as possible against the wall, trying to hide. An eruption of screaming echoes off the walls. The soldiers run through the hut, grabbing women off their shelves and then letting them go so the fun won't end too quickly. Tim's blood turns cold. He clenches his fists as a single tear swells and spills out of the corner of his eye.

Emma's heart pumps ice under her skin as she sees one of the men grab a young girl and quickly carry her out of the hut while she screams. As Kaspar and the other man rummage through the pile of hectic women, Tim hears Emma let out a desperate cry. He yells through the hole, "No! Pretend to be sick, Emma! Remember, cough! Cough!"

Kaspar has plowed through the women and searched the bottom shelves. He halts when he sees Emma. His lazy eyes turn to slits and he sticks his tongue out through his teeth. He grabs Emma, pulling her from her shelf, and drags her while she yells Tim's name.

Tim bangs his fist against the wall.

Emma cries but coughs loudly. She coughs until it feels like rusty nails scratching the inside of her throat and then she coughs some more. She coughs on Kaspar over and over again until he pushes her to the ground in disgust. He wipes his jacket off with his hands and grabs another woman, who balls herself up on the ground in the aisle, and leaves with her. The hut is quiet again, except for muffled sobs for those who were taken.

Tim becomes aware through faint cracks of light that the Jewish men in his hut are leaning out and staring at him.

"I... I'm sorry for shouting."

He can imagine their irritation at being woken from what little sleep they get. After hearing the tears in his voice, however, their faces soften, and they lie back down.

Emma runs back to her shelf and bursts into tears as she buries her head in the wall. Tim puts his mouth directly over the hole. "Emma? You are fine. Listen to me. It's over now. You are safe."

Emma whispers back, "This is too much! I'm too scared."

Tim fights back his tears. "I am right here. You will be all right. I am right here."

Finally Emma's emotions spill out. "They took my wedding ring, Tim! I never sleep! I'm always hungry! My hands are cut and hurt every day!"

Sobbing loudly, she cries, "I am dying. My body is going away. I wouldn't have you see me like this even if you could."

"Don't say that, Emma. You are beautiful to me. You will always be beautiful to me. This won't last—just keep fighting; don't give up."

As Tim's words wash over Emma, her body feels calm again. He continues, "Now you need to sleep. Sleep, and I will be with you again tomorrow night."

Emma whispers, "Thank you."

"Try to get some sleep."

She passes out before the words leave her lips. *"Goodnight, Tim."*

CHAPTER TWELVE

Days become weeks, and weeks become months. It snows regularly now. Tim keeps track of the days by marking the edge of his shelf with a rock. His new life gradually becomes routine, the way the hands of a farmer callous over time. He clamps steel parts together faster than any other captive in the factory, and the Nazis recognize it. Even the Hauptleute has come to observe him work a few times. Under Marcel's order, the Nazis put him in charge of reviewing all the finished products once a week before captives pack them for storage.

If a weapon isn't up to standard, Tim marks the green paper on his clipboard. It keeps him from his shelf an additional hour or two, but the Nazis provide him with an extra loaf of bread in compensation; hardly worth it, but non-negotiable. The first night, he longs for the extra sleep and fights to keep awake, but slowly acclimates to his new task.

No guards watch the door, because the unit has only guns, no ammunition or blades, nothing with which to harm anyone. The first night that Tim tallies, he is surprised to see another captive auditing down the aisle next to him. Tim notices the man's old age before attempting to engage him.

"Hello." Tim shudders. Although brightly lit, the storage space feels much colder than his hut, which he shares with fifty other warm bodies. The unit stretches long, but windowless walls and a low ceiling of bluish-green water pipes makes the room feel as small as a shoebox. Guns lie haphazardly piled on rows of counters for Tim and the other man to tally.

"I haven't seen you before; you must stay in a different hut… do you speak English?" Tim asks.

The elderly black man grunts in German.

"I guess I will translate that as 'no'," Tim mutters under his breath.

After a few moments of silence while the two continue to examine guns and mark their sheets, Tim tries again. "You might not understand me, but I hope you don't mind if I talk to you. At least when I talk with you in the room, it won't be insanity… you wouldn't mind that, would you?" The old man lowers his clipboard and walks toward Tim.

Deep wrinkles cross his forehead like long rivers over bushy white brows. His cheeks sag like empty sacks on either side of his flat nose. His thin white beard would be plush had he not been malnourished. His head is bald, and his fingernails are chipped to the skin. As he moves closer, his dark eyes stare blankly, like one who has lived for many decades yet knows nothing. He reaches quickly and grabs Tim's wrist, picks up a gun, slaps it into his palm, and turns to go back to work.

Tim sets the gun down and laughs. "This job isn't one to take seriously, my friend."

His new partner grimaces and pulls up his shirt to reveal old serial numbers scarred across his chest. Scoffing, Tim lifts his shirt to show his number, too. "This may be you, but it isn't me. I have a name, and it's not this number."

The old man lowers his shirt, his eyes fixed on Tim. "Wie heißen Sie?"

Tim has picked up some German and places his hand on his chest. "Tim."

The man squints and places his hand on his chest, "Udo." Then he turns his back and returns to work.

Rolling his eyes, Tim mumbles, "It's a pleasure to make your acquaintance, Udo."

When both men finish, soldiers escort them in chains to their respective huts. Tim crawls into his shelf. He whispers for Emma through the hole. It is too late; she has gone to sleep. Rupert is still awake in his shelf and he whispers, "How is your new assignment?"

"I still have my old *assignment* with all of you, Rupert."

"Yes, but how is your new one?"

"It was hard. I had to examine each gun and its tag number. If it wasn't a Grade-A, I had to mark it down and list what was wrong with it. I examined hundreds of guns, and I still have thousands left to do."

Rupert slides out of his shelf in surprise, "You do all that by yourself?"

"There was another man who tallied as well, but I was often alone. I believe men from other huts come in to tally at different time during the day, too."

"Why do you say that?"

"There were other marked clipboards with earlier time stamps on them."

"Why don't you fabricate the numbers?" Rupert grunts. "It is wrong to work so hard for Nazis,"

"I agree. It makes me sick knowing I am helping those who keep us here, but I am trying to be safe until I can figure out a way to escape with Emma."

Rupert slides back into his shelf. "It is admirable to place her before yourself like you do. It must be burdensome. I guess I should consider myself lucky in that area, for I have only myself to worry about. I am proud to say that I purposely slack in the factory, it gives me dignity to defy the Nazis under their noses."

Tim inhales deeply. "Do be careful, Rupert."

Drifting off to sleep, Rupert adds, "I sometimes leave the nut loose on the screw for the trigger... sometimes I forget it completely. Imagine a Nazi trying to fire one of those rifles, and there is nothing for his finger to pull on."

Tim shuts his eyes. "Goodnight, Rupert."

Rupert chuckles, "You as well, Tim."

***

Emma takes her seat, as she wills herself to

keep living. She filters through mindless thoughts to try and pass the time, but cannot allow herself to daydream again. The sewing factory is cleaner than the ammunition and firearms portion of the building where Tim works, but it reeks of mold and mildew from the melted snow dripping through the cracks. The sewing machines produce a low rumble, but it isn't loud enough to drown out one's own somber thoughts.

Emma always sits with Johanna and Helene, but there is little left to talk about; most of the time the women work without speaking. They try to find things to say every now and then because the shuffling of hundreds of hands and feet amidst the droning of the machines make one feel she is losing her mind.

This day is like every other until a man walks up behind Emma and stares at her while she works. She stitches, oblivious to the eyes that rest upon her from behind. Suddenly, she feels a warm hand squeeze her shoulder. She jumps in fright and looks up timidly, afraid of being struck. To her surprise, the man smiles. "Are you tired, my dear?"

Emma cannot open her mouth. It is the first time a man other than Tim has spoken to her in English since she has been on the island.

The man gently takes the jacket Emma sews from her hands and says "Please" as he motions her to stand. He smells of fresh linen. The man continues to smile and beckons her to follow him. Emma obediently stays behind him. He leads Emma down two narrow halls and up a short flight of stairs to a thin wooden door. Soldiers stand guard at the entrance to the hallway. She notices that this part of the building is quite well kept.

When the man opens the door and Emma enters what appears to be a well-organized soldier's quarters. A wood fire burns in the wall; it is a small fire, though, for the fireplace seems to have been intended only for decoration. A bed slightly larger than a cot stands made in the corner, but the pillow is crooked, and the covers were left frilled from that morning.

A closed window, nearly five feet from top to bottom, offers a view of the sky outside over the water and the island. A chair that rises high like a throne separates lockers by the wall from a heavy antique work desk inscribed with elaborate designs. Early morning light catches some dirty uniforms spilling out from under the bed.

At first Emma shivers and fidgets nervously, but she soon embraces the warmth the foreign room offers. Once she relaxes, she notices a black candlestick telephone next to a small radio.

"Sit wherever you wish," the man says kindly.

Emma sits down in an armchair facing the desk. The man takes his place in the tall chair. "You must be wondering how I know that you speak English."

Emma remains silent.

The man lifts a manila folder from his desk and grins. He opens it and scans the pages. "You are American. It is a shame to have you here, especially since these papers indicate you are not even a Jew." He does not look up.

Emma's heart pounds but remains silent.

"I have thought for quite some time now about what to do with you. You see, I was your savior that dreadful night," the man says, raising his hand to mimic aiming a rifle and letting off a shot.

Emma's eyes widen as she recalls the image of Ackerman's brain half missing.

"I knew you were American when you arrived, but I had not a clue what to do with you. However, after all this time…" He spreads his hands in the air. "God has given me the answer."

Emma has been looking down, but she looks up expectantly, "Are you releasing me?" Hope surges through her fragile body at the thought of freedom.

The man winces, then immediately feigns a sympathetic frown. "I wish it were that simple. You see, there are not too many who know what is being done here. If I let you go, you might become a tattle-tale. It is like a game, hmm? God is very funny!" He laughs at his own cunning and then fixes his eyes on Emma with an eerie grin. She looks down again to avoid his stare.

The man continues, "You must understand that everything, all this, this factory, these shelters, the Jews, even our interaction now, no one knows of it beyond this island except for my successor. He is starting a program, if you will." He continues proudly, "It will bring Germany to a height of glory the world has never seen."

He leans forward in his chair, resting his weight on his elbows. "I must test it first, in secrecy of course. The Jews we have taken thus far are immigrants, so this beginning stage of operation remains hidden from the world and even my own country for the time being." He reclines backward and smiles. "My successor needs us to perfect the operation before it can be implemented throughout Germany. In other words, you are the first. You should feel honored."

The man pauses, savoring his own words, then stands up and walks towards Emma, his fingers tracing the desk's wooden surface. Standing in front of her, he bows slightly. "I have been rude to you, my apologies. My name is Hauptleute Marcel Wolff."

Marcel extends his hand to Emma until she reluctantly places her hand in his. He leans over and kisses the top of her knuckles. "This is my home, this island. I believe you don't find it home, though, hmm?"

Emma remains silent, but she can tell Marcel especially wants her to answer him this time. She lifts her eyes to meet his. "No, Mr. Wolff."

"Ah, now we are having a conversation. This is the only thing that keeps us civil. And you are so honest, too. However, I wish to know what it is that keeps this from being your home? I have given you food, water, a bed. I am your provider."

Emma looks down at her torn clothes and shuts her eyes. "You mock me."

"I could not be more sincere. You would be dead here if not for me. The work is hard, I understand, but how could you be upset with God's will?"

Emma glances up at Marcel, weak but tense inside.

Now sitting behind his desk again, Marcel leans back with his fingers steepled together. "It isn't the work that kills you. You are a strong one. A strength you learned I can see. It is the random fear at night... my men. Am I correct?"

Emma turns away. Marcel stands and walks to his window, placing his hand against the cold glass.

"You can see your hut from here, my dear," he points out.

Emma stays quiet.

Marcel removes his hand from the glass, leaving a silhouette of condensation. He rubs the mark of water away and looks across the glimmering snow and clear grey sky. "My men get lonely here. You can understand. They tend to be, however... impolite about it." Turning to look at Emma, he states, "I myself do not share their manners."

He walks over to her and takes both of her hands in his. Emma wants to jerk away and command him not to touch her. She wants to scream for Tim to come rescue her, yet all she can do in defiance is look away and remain silent.

Marcel stares at her until she looks back at him. His eyes bore through her as he speaks. "Someone as beautiful as you should be courted."

With his fingertips, he slowly strokes the skin on her hands. Emma's eyes well up with tears. She hates that he touches her. She looks him straight in the eyes and says, "You are mad if you perceive the bones and flesh of this walking corpse you've created as beautiful."

Marcel laughs, "So it is food you desire. Of that I have plenty." He walks to a cabinet and pulls out fresh pastries and fruits and places them on the desk.

"Or perhaps it is warmth you long for? Like a bath," Marcel then opens the door to his lavatory with its spotless porcelain tub. Emma tries to remain stoic, but she blushes with fury. He walks over to her chair, placing his hands on the armrests as he leans over her.

"I will have you," Marcel whispers in a deep voice.

Tears run down Emma's face. She looks at Marcel. "Well, go on! You're already joining your men on the same track to hell as it is!"

Marcel takes his hands off the chair and stands erect. "Oh no, my dear, that is where you are wrong. You will accept me willingly." He reaches for the food he laid out on his desk and slowly slides it towards Emma.

Refusing to look at the food, Emma announces through her quivering lips, "I would rather die on this island than give in to…"

Before she has time to finish, Marcel pounds his desk with a fist. Then he screams with a red face, "You will give yourself to me!"

Turning his back on her, he walks over to his chair and plops down.

Concerned German voices come through the

door—the soldiers are asking if they should enter and aid Marcel. He orders them in and motions for them to escort Emma away. He stares viciously at her while the soldiers take her.

As the soldiers drag Emma through the door, Marcel shouts for his men to halt. Still sitting at his desk, he dabs a feather into ink next to a brass paper-weight bust of a stallion.

Marcel writes busily, then puts the pen away and rises from his chair. He walks over to the soldiers, pulls Emma from their hands, and pushes them out into the hallway. He shuts the door and inhales deeply as his hand remains on the knob. Emma barely breathes as she waits for Marcel's next move. Her vision blurs with black spots as her heart thumps hard against her chest.

Marcel turns around and smiles at her. He steps towards her with outstretched arms. Leaning his forehead into her, he slides his arms around her waist.

Emma lets out a long cry and nearly chokes on her own anguish as Marcel sways with her in his arms.

"I don't mean to frighten you, my dear," he says softly. He leans back, wrapping his hands tightly around Emma's face.

Closing his eyes, he takes a deep breath and exhales. "When I was but a boy, my father had two wire-haired pointer puppies, one midnight black and the other spotted grey and white. He needed to raise hunting dogs to fetch his grouse and duck. I never seem to remember the name of the black dog, but the adorable spotted one was named Barco; I remember because I named him."

Emma sniffles and tugs a bit to see if Marcel will let her slip to a more comfortable distance, but her attempt meets with resistance.

"My father never loved either of the dogs, but he never loved anyone, not even Mother."

Emma tries to think of Tim, but the blood pounding through her head blocks happy thoughts. She can think only of a way to escape. She remembers the rifle Marcel used to shoot Ackerman—it must be lying in the room somewhere.

"There was a problem with both dogs after they had matured... neither of them would obey Father when he commanded them to go and fetch his kill. He sought to remedy the situation by bringing sweetmeats with him to bribe the dogs into fetching." Marcel looks off to the side. "This worked like a charm for the black dog, but Barco was..." he shakes his head disappointedly, "stubborn. Even after taking the meats he would still not obey Father."

Emma grabs Marcel's wrists. She tries with her little strength to loosen his grip, but he squeezes even tighter.

"Instead of retrieving fowl," Marcel continues, "Barco would chase his tail, or be led astray by his nose from the peculiar odors of the woods, or he would lick the flowers." He chuckles. "Barco enjoyed the fuzzy feeling of the bluebottle's petals on his tongue the most."

The pounding in Emma's head becomes unbearable. The muscles in her legs shake, but she fights to keep her knees from buckling. Unable to pry loose of Marcel's grip, her arms merely hang like ornaments.

"Father wanted to whip Barco until he was frightened into obedience. My loving mother, however, would not permit that." Marcel closes his eyes and smiles.

"You might say that Mother's love kept Barco from the whip. So, the question then arose, how do you get a dog to obey, when you have neither a carrot nor a stick…? Hmm? Or maybe just shoot it dead? Give up; perhaps let it loose into nature?" Marcel releases his grip to stroke Emma's face gently—immediately, tears pour down her cheeks.

"Well, Father developed a solution," he says with a finger pointed in the air. "Do you know what he did?" Emma bites her lip and looks down to see if Marcel has a knife or a pistol on his belt. There is an empty pistol holster, but no sheath for a knife.

She shakes her head.

"One wet, thunderous night, he took Barco and me into the forest and tied Barco to a tree. Father pulled me away from Barco and told me to watch. Barco looked around with fear and tried to wiggle away but the ropes were too tight. He looked at me for help, but I was only to watch."

Emma looks up at Marcel. Her body fidgets but her head remains still. She stares into his eyes and realizes, *I'm Barco…*

"Father then took a hatchet to the dog's flesh, cutting off his tail, his nose, and even cutting out his tongue. It was dark and raining, and Father was quick to bandage the dog's wounds, but I still remember Barco's white spots turning dark red from his blood."

Emma's lips quiver and she grows cold all over.

"The next time father went hunting, he commanded Barco to join the black dog in gathering his kill. Stubborn Barco looked to chase his tail first but found only a nub. He then sought to lick the colorful bluebottle petals he loved so much but tasted no more than air. Finally, he ran off to lose himself in the scents of the forest, sniffing all around, trying to smell the tall pines and rich dirt, but it was in vain."

Emma forgets all about escaping from Marcel's room. She forgets about Tim, her family, her pain. She looks around the room and longs for her life to end.

Then Marcel winks. "Barco looked at my father and trotted into the fields to fetch the kill from then on."

Marcel regains his grip on Emma's face before continuing. "Both dogs eventually listened to my father, but Barco was left without the things he loved." A long pause snatches the sound from the room as he stares into Emma's wide blue eyes before she squeezes them shut. "I will find out what it is you love more than me, and I will take it from you. I will be the one who takes love from your life, leaving you with nothing but obedience." He slaps Emma across the face, cutting her cheek with his gold ring.

Emma winces and jerks her head away, but Marcel grabs her face again. Holding her by both cheeks, he sighs, "Oh dear, look what a mess you made me cause," when he sees her blood on his hand.

Releasing her and reaching for the doorknob, he takes out a handkerchief to wipe his hands. Shaking with fear, Emma stands alone in the room. Marcel opens the door and motions for her to leave. She returns to the hallway, expecting at any moment to be snatched back into his sadistic torment.

As the door slams behind her, she doubles over, grabbing her stomach. She shakes and closes her eyes as the soldiers escort her back to the factory.

Seated again at her machine, Johanna leans over to Emma and asks, "What did the Hauptleute want?"

Emma doesn't respond, but instead looks around the factory. She looks at all the somber faces of the tired and fearful women. Then she looks directly at Johanna. "He is going to hurt Tim."

Johanna looks away to think about what this means. Emma reaches out and turns her friend's face toward her. The two young women look deeply into each other's eyes. "Johanna... will you help me kill the Hauptleute?"

CHAPTER THIRTEEN

The evening after her encounter with Marcel, Emma kneels by her shelf with her forehead resting on her crossed arms. Women in the hut talk amongst themselves, caring for one another's wounds, especially those who are weakest. E lies on her shelf, studying Emma until she finally comes out and places her hand on Emma's shoulder.

"I am sorry, Mauseäbar, is everything alright with you? You have been praying for a long time now."

"Yes, everything is fine, I am not praying, I am thinking," Emma says.

"About?"

Emma looks at her with a stern countenance.

E's eyes widen, and she kneels beside Emma. "No! I have told you before, it is nonsense. There is no escaping this place."

Emma brushes E's hand away and stands up. "And why is that? Tell me! I am not able to fathom a reason why we all cannot leave this place. There are boats that come and go, why can we not sneak on one of those or something of the kind?"

E slowly shakes her head. "Mauseäbar, the only thing leaving on those boats are dead bodies, victims of this island, especially the Raupe. My heart would perish if I saw you on one of those boats. Please, a day will come where we will be delivered from this island, but let it come in its own time."

Emma cocks her head. "What did you say?"

"We will be delivered... soon," E repeats.

"No, the name of that building. I had forgotten what it's called... what is its name again?"

"Raupe."

Emma ponders the name. "How does it work?"

"I have only heard stories, but it is a kind of poison, I believe. The Nazis put us inside of it and then douse us."

"Poison?"

"Mausebär, what does it matter? You will never enter the Raupe, you will stay safe, do you understand?"

Emma looks away. "I understand."

***

The next morning, Emma sits and sews next to Johanna and Helene. Johanna sits in the middle.

"Ach!" Johanna shouts after stabbing her finger with a sewing pin.

Emma looks at the injury, but when she sees it's only a small prick, she continues with her own work. She pauses a moment, however, to think.

"How long have you worked in the sewing room?" she asks Johanna.

Johanna sucks on her finger. "Since I have been here."

"Are there no other jobs outside the sewing room for you?"

"Yes, but they are not as good. Only the kitchen is better." Johanna wipes her finger on her blouse.

Emma leans forward. "Yes, the kitchen. Why do you not work there? I'm sure your soldier could move you."

"I don't know. I was just put here. Now I have become used to it," Johanna responds.

"Would you not rather work in the kitchen?"

"I don't know." Johanna shrugs her shoulders and looks at Emma. "Why do you ask?"

Emma notices a guard staring at them, so she quickly goes back to sewing, "Because…" Emma first says too loudly, and then repeats herself in a whisper, "because, do you remember when I asked you to help me with the Hauptleute?"

"I remember," Johanna answers. Helene leans over to listen to the conversation.

"Well, I have become familiar with how you can help. Ask your soldier if you can work another job, any other job. Preferably the kitchen, because you said it is better."

"How does that help you kill the Hauptleute?" Johanna asks.

Emma looks at Johanna. "*Us*, Johanna, it will help *us* kill him, and because I don't know of anyone else outside the sewing factory except for E. She works in the medical area and the laundry, but I cannot ask for her help to do this."

"But how does that help?" Johanna persists.

"Because there is poison in this building, the same poison used for... for the Raupe," Emma says in a whisper.

Johanna and Helene lean forward to listen better. "The path we take from the huts to the sewing factory does not pass any doors. If we find a door, then we find a room; if we find a room, then we have a chance of finding where the poison is," Emma explains.

"What kind of poison?" Johanna asks. Helena nods to affirm Johanna's question.

"I am not certain. All I know is that it is the poison the Nazis use in the Raupe."

Helena's eyes widen, and she shakes with excitement. She looks like she wants to speak, but she only pats the table and points around. The commotion draws the eyes of a few captives, but Johanna quickly pulls her sister's hands down, and says, "Hör auf verrückt zu sein, Helena."

Helena turns swiftly to her sewing kit. She grabs some blue thread and rolls it up into a ball the size of a pea. She repeats this process until she has four rolls. She holds one up, pretends to swallow it, and grabs her throat and mimics a cough before pretending to die.

Emma's eyes widen. "You know what the poison is?"

Helene nods.

Johanna sees two Nazis looking over at them, so she quickly goes back to sewing and subtly motions for the others to do the same. When the two Nazis move on to patrol other women, Emma whispers, "Johanna, can you ask your soldier to station Helena in the kitchen?"

Johanna leans back, away from Emma and stares straight ahead. "What does being in the kitchen have to do with getting to the Hauptleute?"

"I need help finding the poison and spreading out does that," Emma says.

Johanna hesitates. "Very well, I will see what I can do."

CHAPTER FOURTEEN

Winter settles in, and the sun's path in the sky becomes less and less noticeable to the captives. The island has taken ground in the mind of every captive, shrinking their concern for life down to the size of a grain of sand—a grain that would simply brush off one's shoulder from a light breeze, that would get caught under a fingernail only to be washed out and left to drift down a drain.

At first the Jews felt their capture was punitive and important, but when every day shows that the ocean is as barren as the day before, they begin to feel insignificant. Their demise was never punitive or purposeful; it was flippant. The horizon never brings ships with heroes coming to free them, God seems to be more distant than the stars, and desolate weeks pour into a constant flow with no end in sight.

Waking in the morning becomes so routine that one cannot distinguish this day from the next. The first thought every Jew wakes to is that they are still alive, that they still exist, if only barely. This thought recycles so often that it feels like the first thought each captive has ever had in their lives, a déjà vu of their own inception. The realization of barely existing runs through Emma's mind, scrubbing away her memories. Hope is whitewashed over time and reaching for the heavens soon becomes too wearisome for sore shoulders.

The weight of an entirely absent world crushes Emma, especially when she sews, a skill passed down to her from her mother. Sewing for the Nazis, however, is much different than when she learned it. She works without a thimble, and it is hurried. As a young girl, she spent hours carefully laying the pieces together as her mother pinned the edges tightly. They would talk and laugh as they recounted stories of relatives coming to visit, or recipes that did not turn out quite as expected. Now her hands are frightened into working the needle quicker than her mind can function, and for longer than her eyes can stay open, but she manages all the same—all the women do.

Tim again finds himself tallying rifles at the end of another week. His mind is numb from long hours of work at the factory. He keeps blinking his eyes and shaking his head trying to focus as he makes each mark on his green sheet.

Tim is not too tired, however, to notice Udo working diligently, which makes him pause and chuckle. His laugh turns into a long yawn before he goes back to tallying. After a while Udo has almost finished his row of rifles for the night, yet Tim is barely half finished. Before Tim can realize he slacks,

Udo quietly walks over to one of Tim's rows and begins checking and tallying with him.

"What are you doing?"

Udo keeps working as if he doesn't hear. Tim shrugs his shoulders."Danke."

When the two men finish for the night, Udo unclips three sheets of paper from his clipboard and hands them to Tim so that he will receive full credit for the section assigned to him. Udo then hangs his board on the wall and knocks on the door to let the guards know they are finished.

The soldiers come in and cuff both men. Tim stares at Udo the whole time, realizing he has never asked about Udo's story... how he was captured and brought to the island. Walking outside Tim notices a few Nazis by the Raupe, thinking to himself, *They must be preparing it for use soon.*

In the middle of the night, the walls rumble from a snowstorm that blows in off the water. Ice clinks and bashes against the roof, forcing the famished and exhausted men to stay awake. Tim knows Emma cannot be sleeping through the storm, so he tries to talk to her through the wall, but the pounding drowns out his voice.

On the other side of the wall, Emma huddles with the other women in the back of her hut while the walls shake. As always, she prays and hopes Tim is safe. The fierce storm frightens the women, but Emma thinks of Tim and stays calm. She closes her eyes and remembers when she was taken from him by the Nazis and felt that she had lost him forever.

Locked in the bottom of the boat, the heavy cloak of loneliness wrapped itself around her. Yet even in despair, the thought of Tim brought her comfort.

The first days were the hardest. Learning to sleep on the hard shelf robbed her mind of sanity. She was slow to adjust to the harsh living, trying to endure but all the while remembering her large warm house with its velvet curtains and soft bed. Constant hunger, even after a meal, eventually became normal.

With the passage of time—days turning into weeks, and weeks turning into months—cold, hunger and pain are normal now, and, though it is never spoken of, every passing day seems to be one tick closer to death. Emma, however, still dreams each day of being home again. She knows that her thoughts are critical, so she thinks of Tim and can feel his strong arms around her shoulders.

The storm rages into the wee hours. Tim lies awake, wondering if even the Nazis could be cruel enough to make a man work after a sleepless night like this.

Before sunrise the door of Tim's hut swings open as usual, letting in a blast of overpowering cold that flushes out what little heat had been created during the night. As his eyes creak open, he becomes aware of how desperately his body needs rest. He can't remember the storm subsiding or dreaming at all.

At the angry cries of the Nazi soldiers, who were also unable to sleep, the sluggish captives climb out of their shelves and stand in line. The Nazis lead

Tim and the prisoners outside, but instead of turning toward the dark building, they are directed to the edge of the island where the water meets land.

Each step they take sinks shin-deep as the cold burns their skin. The air is still. The men trudge silently, only exhaling puffs like smoke from a small doused fire. The Nazis eventually order the men to halt. As they stand shivering, soldiers throw blankets upon their backs. Tim feels the rough dun-colored cloth drape around him. It smells like a feral animal and has holes he can put his arms through where moths have gorged themselves, offering little warmth.

After lining up the prisoners shoulder to shoulder, the soldiers shout orders through the freezing air. Tim tries to interpret the commands as the head officer orders the Jews to fix the damaged fence on the west side of the island.

In the low light of dawn Tim perceives how mangled the cage around the island became after the storm. The fence is now all but completely gone after the thrashing of the waves, winds, and ice. All around, the wire is either bent over or lying flat in the snow, waiting to be propped back up and fortified.

Tim peers across the land and over the silent waters. He imagines himself tossing the blanket off his back and making a run for it, but his hope of diving off the island into freedom sinks with the realization that the sea is deep and virtually everlasting. Tim shakes his head. The hope of escape slips away like a wave sliding down the shore, back into the sea.

Before long the men are hard at work clearing the destroyed fence, bringing fresh metal and barbed wire from storage, and mending it all. They spend hours building their new cage. Men fall on their faces in exhaustion from the work. Some are beaten and propped back up while others are taken away. Their lifeless bodies leave gouged paths in the snow.

The old metal blackens noses and fingers while wire cuts jagged wounds into sensitive flesh. The captives move like the undead. Although their wrists are free to work, nearly all lose feeling in their feet from the iced rusty metal that links to chains around their ankles and freezes to their skin.

Morning light finally crests the horizon, but utterly fails to inspire the workers. The number of total captives surprises Tim when he looks around. He doesn't know if all the men he sees have been on the island since he arrived, or if the camp has been quietly growing in his sleep.

Tim holds down a metal beam for other men to wire when his eyes catch the sunlight glistening on the surface of the water, and in an instant, his mind takes him away. He is with Emma. She is asleep on a clean-white bed that seems to rest on a cloud. Her legs are bare as she wears his favorite blue collared shirt which covers just past her upper thigh.

Tim brushes her forehead with his hand while her eyes are closed, lifting a few soft blond hairs from her face. He bends down to kiss her but feels his nose and cheeks burn sharp with cold. A Nazi stuns him and brings him back to the island where he finds himself lying face first in the snow. An angry knee twists in his back.

The soldier shoving his kneecap deep into Tim's spine shrieks with laughter and strikes him across his ear with the back of his hand, then hoists Tim up to his hands and knees.

The soldier pushes Tim's head towards the fence on the ground and screams at him in German. Tim blows what breath he has onto his numb hands and then presses down on the cold pole again. While pressing the beam, he cocks his head to the side where he sees other captives smiling at his demise. Seeing others find humor in his discipline is concerning, but Tim has neither the time nor strength to consider what it means.

Focusing his attention on the frozen pole, he holds it firmly in place. He feels a chill in his bones, as if the metal has become one with his body. As Tim tries to distract himself from the pain, he notices something small sticking up from the snow an arm's length away. It is a long blade of grass.

Looking around to make sure no one is watching, he reaches for it. It is longer than his forearm, but no thicker than the width of a fingernail. Plucking the blade from the ground, Tim has an urge to eat it before he realizes it is probably dead and therefore nutritionally worthless.

The grass on the island is peculiar, scarce, and present only where no footsteps tread. After a moment, two soldiers approach Tim who quickly bends the reed and hides it under his blanket. He holds his breath in anticipation of the Nazis' suspicion but sighs with relief as they pass by without a glance.

Work slows the hours of the day to near stagnation as the men finish the fence the best they can. Then the soldiers lead them in a line around the dark building to the other side of the island. The Jews' hearts sink to their empty stomachs when they see that they are only halfway done with the fence. As the soldiers escort the captives to the remnants of the rest of the cage, Tim realizes he is on the other side of his hut, which means he is now looking at the front of the women's barracks. His heart begins to pump faster as he comes closer and closer to Emma's hut. There is a small square hole on every door just like on his.

Tim counts off each door he passes until he reaches Emma's. He begins to sweat and shake, but he can't let this chance go. When he gets in front of the door, he leans out of line and peeks through the hole. It is no use. The moving line gives him only a second to look, but it's too dark inside to see within. A few men mutter complaints about him tugging the chains. Tim quickly falls back in line.

Upon reaching the other side of the island, the prisoners resume their work. Although they are never enthusiastic about their drudgery, this session seems to be greeted with exceptional distaste and duress. Freshly demoralized at the thought of missing a chance to see Emma, Tim consoles himself by thinking that the women had probably left for the factory at that time, so he had not missed an actual opportunity to see her.

Soon Tim is sent with a few dozen men far down the edge of the island. They are to start gathering the destroyed fence where it connects to the part that still stands. He notices that Rupert is now by his side and smiles. Tim gets closer to his friend as they walk beside each other in silence.

While the captives in Tim's group work, some soldiers separate a few men and take them to get more metal, leaving just a small number of soldiers watching over Tim and the others.

As Tim folds some torn metal fencing in order to compact it for carrying, he sees a small wrecked boat in the harbor. Snow nearly covers it. He assumes it must have crashed ashore during the storm and yells and points to it until a soldier comes to see why he is being disruptive.

When the Nazi spies the boat, he orders Tim and Rupert to examine it. They trek down in the cold and push the snow off of the boat only to discover that it is damaged beyond repair. Tim assumes it was either pulled loose from a harbor or the captain was tossed aside during the storm. Either way, it is useless.

The Nazi watches them. As soon as Tim and Rupert wave to report that there is nothing to find, the soldier orders other captives to help push the boat out into the water. The weak men heave and strain to shove the craft off the island.

Once the men set the small boat free, they watch it sail off into the sea before turning back. Tim watches it drift under the rising sun as a cold breeze crosses his face. He is already cold but still enjoys the sensation, until something catches his eye. A black rock floats in the water a few meters from where he stands. He crouches to inspect it and then looks down to see that his feet stand on similar material. He picks up a piece of the ground and tosses it out. This rock bobs on the surface as well.

Tim whispers to himself, "Volcanic... porous."

Walking back to join the others, he sees a bit of rope lying in the snow from the wrecked boat. Without thinking, he ties it around his waist and then pulls his blanket around his body to keep it concealed. He walks back behind the other men. Rupert, witnessing this subterfuge, whispers, "Tim, what are you doing? You can't sneak something like that past the guards."

Tim grins. "You are right. I'm going to bury it outside the gate when I get the chance."

The other prisoners show up with new metal and wire. Tim sees an older man who is carrying metal beams slowly losing his grip and goes over to help him.

As they walk together Tim feels the rope come loose around his waist. He presses the rope against his hip to keep it from becoming visible. When he does, the beams fall and clank onto the ground. A soldier spins around and sees Tim's guilty face. He races over, raising his boots high above the snow with each step.

When the officer reaches Tim, he punches him in the face. Tim falls to the ground, imprinting the snow with his body. With a snarl, the soldier commands him to pick up the beams. Tim complies. As they clank back together, a few of the captives snicker at him again.

Hours pass, and the sun begins to descend. As the men finish the new fence they drip with cold sweat. A soldier gives the fence a sturdy shake and motions for the men to shackle up again.

A commander shouts that the work day is still not finished. The captives must now go into the factory. Men collapse, wishing for death rather than more work. Soldiers strike those who fall until they stand up again.

Tim has left a clamp unattached to the fence. As the men march, he spits the clamp from his mouth into the snow and steps on it to hide it. When the captives enter the building, the soldiers strip them of their blankets. When Tim's blanket flies off, Rupert sees he has on nothing but his tattered rags.

As the men enter the factory, they all sigh. They are happy to be out of the snow, but distraught to still be working.

CHAPTER FIFTEEN

The night after the brutal storm, Tim and his fellow prisoners enter their hut and lie heavily in their shelves with more aches and pains than ever before. He lies still for a moment to embrace the relaxation. Then he taps the wall behind him and whispers, "Hey, Beautiful."

Emma whispers back, "Hey! How did you keep last night?"

"It wasn't unbearable. You?"

Emma forces a smile. "It wasn't unbearable."

"Are you still staying strong for me?"

Emma smiles again. "You know I am. How about you?"

"Always."

After a slight pause, Tim whispers, "I am sorry for getting you here, Emma. It wasn't fair to you. It wasn't just of me."

"Don't apologize. This isn't your fault."

Tim stares at the bottom of Rupert's shelf. "I feel guilt."

"Well, don't," Emma answers toughly.

Tim smiles again. "So, you still trust me?"

"Always."

Tim air-kisses the wall loud enough for Emma to hear it. "Get some sleep, Emma."

Emma responds, "I love you, Tim. Goodnight." She lays her head down with a smile on her face.

Tim whispers back, "I love you, too."

After about an hour of lying awake, Tim hears Rupert whisper, "Tim? Tim, are you sleeping?"

Tim inhales heavily and says, "I am awake."

"I wish to ask…"

As Rupert speaks, Tim feels a pair of bony hands wring his neck. He gasps for air as he kicks the attacker backward and rolls out of his shelf onto the cold dirt floor.

Standing up, a man tackles him to the ground and punches him repeatedly. Tim raises his arms to block the blows, but many land regardless. The prisoner fights like an insane man.

All the men watch from their shelves like spectators in an arena. Rupert, however, springs from his shelf and pries the crazed man off. Tim scuttles back against the wall as Rupert pins the man, yelling at him in German to calm down. A few other men leave their shelves to help suppress the lunatic.

It is dark, but Tim can see the anger on the man's face. The captive eventually calms down, and the men let him go. He spits on the ground and returns to his shelf. Some of the men who assisted Rupert look back at Tim and shake their heads before moving back to their shelves as well.

Rupert offers Tim a hand up. As he rises, Tim asks, "What happened?"

Rupert's face grows sullen. "Work."

"What do you mean 'work'?"

"I did not wish to say anything, but you work faster than the rest, Tim, and the Nazis always notice. You have been making the rest of us look deficient. You are oblivious to it since all of the talking in this place isn't in your tongue."

Tim approaches Rupert's shelf aggressively. "What are you talking about?"

Rupert explains, "I watched that man get beaten the other day in the factory. A soldier asked him why he works so slow to which he answered that he was tired. The Nazi screamed at him and pointed to you. I guess he said that he should work like you, even though he is tired. Then the soldier hit him with his gun many times."

Tim's mouth hangs open. "I can't accept that I would ever cause more hardship for anyone here." He grabs Rupert by the collar. "Why haven't you told me this? Was it your plan to wait for a man to snap like tonight?"

Rupert grabs Tim's wrists and says, "I was letting you play safe, the way you desire. Had I told you this you would slack because of it... who knows what repercussions could have been for you."

"My life isn't worth any more than anyone else's."

Rupert lays his hand on Tim's shoulder and speaks gently. "None of our lives are worth anything in here, American. Maybe yours isn't either, but there is woman on the other side of this wall. Her life is worth something. This is no place for a woman, especially your wife, the way you speak of her."

Tim stares down at his bare feet in the dark. "What should I do then? I will not have men beaten, or even killed because of me."

Rupert answers, "I am sorry, friend."

The following morning Tim enters the factory. The men post at their stations and begin their shifts for the day with heavy hands. Today Tim notices the glares of the others around him.

He sits on his stool and pieces a rifle together. He has trained his hands so well that he can do it blindfolded. His hands no longer cramp and the muscles in his forearms stay loose for hours. He looks around the factory at all the men and thinks of what might happen to any of them if he continues to show the Nazis how fast he can work with little bread, food, or sleep. He debates whether to keep working as he has, which he now sees as selfish. He thinks of gradually working more slowly but shakes his head. He weighs the repercussions for himself and all the other men in the balance.

Finally, his face relaxes, and he sets a rifle down. He shuts his eyes tightly and balls his hands into fists. Tim feels the blood pulse through the veins in his eyes as a single bead of sweat trickles down his face. He inhales deeply.

With a shaky hand, he stands up and abruptly pushes all the guns and parts on his table onto the floor. The noisy machines keep many from hearing what he does, but it is too blatant to go completely unseen. Tim looks up to see two soldiers pacing towards him.

He waits for the Nazis to come closer and then pushes the gun parts on either side of himself onto the ground as well. The prisoners sitting by Tim back away in shock. The men all around watch without moving. The soldiers run towards the mess. The men on either side of Tim lift their hands in innocence while the soldiers stand before him with open mouths.

"You do?" one of the soldiers shouts.

Tim remains silent. He bows his head and shuts his eyes. Nazis and captives all around the factory are watching now.

One soldier yells at Tim to pick up the mess. He remains standing silently by his seat. The soldier grabs Tim and squeezes his neck with powerful fingers. Tim clenches his jaw in pain but doesn't move. The two soldiers look at each other in enraged disbelief.

One soldier hands the other his gun and punches Tim in the back of the head. He hits the floor with a hard thud. The soldier kicks him in his stomach and ribs until he decides Tim has received enough punishment. It is likely that the beating would have been worse had Tim not been who he was in the Nazis' eyes.

The soldier then tries to drag him back up to the table. Tim stubbornly lies heavily on the floor. This irritates the Nazi, who resumes striking him all over. The soldier alternates his punches between

Tim's face and stomach so that if he chooses to protect one, the other is sure to be hit. The blows come rapidly, and Tim wheezes from the pain.

Thin strands of oxygen struggle to enter Tim's lungs through his bloody air pipes. The man tortures Tim with his fists until his knuckles become sore. Then he switches to his boots. The Nazi's kicks are less frequent than the punches but twice as painful. Every eye is turned towards the show now. The entire factory is a witness to Tim's punishment.

Tim senses his spirit wanting to leave his body because the pain is unbearable. He reaches out in a plea for mercy, but his hand is slapped away, and his face struck again.

The Nazi has blood all over his uniform. Tim quivers on the ground as the exhausted soldier walks over to his comrade and takes back his rifle. In his anger he is ready to shoot him and end his life. Tim raises his hand upon the rifle and weakly lowers the barrel from pointing at his head. The Nazi shakes Tim's hand off. Tim's eyes roll back in his head and then shut. He gasps, "Emma..."

The soldier places his boot on Tim's head to hold him down. Prisoners all around the dark factory see one of their own about to die. None of the captives are able to stop what is happening and none of the soldiers care to stop it.

Tim gurgles, "Please," as the panting soldier cocks his gun and puts his finger on the trigger.

Suddenly, a roaring shout bellows from atop the corner balcony. Every eye looks up to see who gave the command. Tim barely looks up at his rescuer and then all goes black as he passes out.

CHAPTER SIXTEEN

One week after Emma asked Johanna for her help to relocate Helena, she sits at her sewing wheel with only Johanna beside her.

"I did it," Johanna says.

There is now a woman other than Helena sewing next to her and Johanna.

"Helena is in the kitchen now?" Emma asks.

Johanna nods.

Emma exhales softly. "Good. Good. Now we have to find out what she sees on her way to the kitchen every day. Doors, hallways, crates of some kind, anything that could help us."

Johanna only grunts in response. Emma looks directly at her. "You should be thankful I am encouraging for us to escape this place. You can't honestly say you want to stay here forever?"

"Hmpf," Johanna responds. "This place is not so bad as it could be."

Emma's lip curls and she looks down at her sewing. She blurts sharply, "Oh, you will see! When I get us out of here, you'll be unable to control your gratitude."

The two women sew in awkward silence for

several minutes. Finally, Emma says, "I am sorry."

Johanna glares at her, then at her sewing wheel. She holds up the trousers she has made to check her work.

CHAPTER SEVENTEEN

Tim wakes up abruptly and knocks his head on something hard; it is the bottom of Rupert's shelf. He reaches up to touch his throbbing skull and feels his head wrapped thick with gauze. The intense pain is overwhelmed by the shock of finding himself alive and back in the hut. Tim wants to get up but realizes he physically can't. He simply lies in his shelf and rests.

An hour passes, and the hut door opens. Tim squints as the light from outside shines directly in his eyes. He recognizes Marcel, who enters with a guard carrying a wooden chair. The moment Marcel sees Tim looking at him, he announces in his strong German accent, "Ah, you are awake this time! I was beginning to think you might sleep there forever. That would have been a shame. All my efforts to keep you alive would have been in vain."

Marcel approaches like a hunter who has shot a prized animal. He speaks in German to the accompanying soldier, who places the chair on the floor, then turns and leaves the hut.

"You gave us quite a show in there this morning," Marcel says with a smile.

Tim regards the man in silence, too nervous to speak.

Marcel continues, "How are your wounds? Come now, let me see them. Come out into the light so I can see you better."

Tim's bruised ribs and damaged abdomen make it painful to move an inch, but he leans out as far as he can. Marcel's smile freezes as he repeats slowly, "Come... out... into... the light."

Tim grimaces as he obeys the command. He manages to get out of his shelf. He strains while propping himself up to stand before Marcel.

"Ah, there you are! You are strong, American, very strong. How do you feel? Ready to walk back into the factory?"

Tim's bloodshot eyes widen in fright at the thought of working in such a wretched condition. Fear sends chills down his back, and his knees wobble. Upon seeing his reaction, Marcel throws his head back in laughter. "Come now, don't be ridiculous. That would kill even you, I suppose... correct, American?"

Tim shuts his eyes, fighting back tears as he realizes how helpless he is. He wants to thank Marcel for not making him work, but hates himself for thinking such a thought, for wanting to thank the man who holds his life in the palm of his hand without letting go.

Suddenly, Tim realizes his mind has drifted. He hears Marcel asking again, "Correct, American?"

Having forgotten the question, and not wanting to upset Marcel, he says, "Yes." Marcel smiles and walks back to his wooden chair.

"That is something I don't think you fully understand. All I must do is say the word, and your life is no more. I don't want to do that, though... you tally well, very few mistakes missed." Marcel pauses to admire his own benevolence. Then he stands up with his nose only a few centimeters from Tim's. He places his hand on Tim's waist and grins.

"Just remember, American, no matter how much I fancy you... everyone is replaceable on my island." While Marcel speaks, he digs his fingers into Tim's injured ribs, causing him to grimace in pain. "Everyone..."

When he lets go, Tim falls to the floor and holds his ribs. Marcel grabs his chair and drags it out of the room, whistling with every step. He locks the door behind him. Tim is alone again. He stays on the ground. He hasn't enough strength to get back in his shelf.

Tim lies on the ground until the darkness of night encroaches upon the hut. Clinging to life, he crawls over to the brick wall and sits upright, but he is unable to climb into his shelf. He sits for a moment until he hears the door in the women's hut behind him open. He waits until he thinks Emma has reached her shelf in the back, then whispers loud enough through the crack, "Hey, Beautiful."

"Tim?" Emma's voice rings with worry. "How did you get back here so soon? What is happening?"

Tim smiles. The sound of her voice is sweet, and her tenderness refreshes his aching soul. "I have been working extra and finished early today." Emma doesn't understand but inquires no further.

"Emma, do you know what today is?"

Emma ponders the question for a moment and answers, "No... I lost track of time a while ago, Timmy."

Tim reaches into his thin excuse for a pillow and pulls out a green sheet of paper, giving it a quick final evaluation and then rolling it into a thin tube. Straining to lift his sore shoulder, Tim reaches up to the hole in the wall and pushes it through. Emma sees a bit of the paper stick through her side and catches hold of it with her fingertips before pulling it through. "What is this? How did you get paper?" she asks.

"I tally the storage, remember? Read it."

Emma unrolls the sheet in the failing light of her hut and reads.

You may think yourself a withered girl,
As if the mirror shows a dull flower,
These words will hang that lie up to unfurl;
To show your beauty's blossom is forever.

The azalea's slender stem dreams of you,
To have a shape as beautiful as yours.
Jealous pretty petals cry tears of dew,
At how your eyes mesmerize like the tides of shores.

My azalea, your pink cheeks blush bright,
Your lips bloom vivid when they smile.
Your azure eyes rival nature's daylight
Along a still stare, fair and fragile.

Your grace is perennial, a charm specific to you.
The mirror is a lie; trust my words are true.

P.S. Happy Birthday, Love.

Tears stream down Emma's face. "How did you remember in this hellish place?" she sobs uncontrollably. She wipes her cheeks with her tattered gown. "This was dangerous. You didn't have to do this for me!"

Tim smiles. "That's what happens when you are loved. You don't have to ask. One just does it because they love you."

Emma tries to stop her crying, but it is in vain. She has been uncontrollably elated a number of times in her life, and all have been due to Tim.

Trying to gain control, she scolds, "You are mad if you think this poem describes me."

Tim keeps a straight face and answers quickly, "I am mad. I am madly in love with you. I always will be."

She laughs through her tears. "I love this so much, Tim. It is wonderful."

"You're welcome, Beautiful, but that's not all."

Emma whispers, "What do you mean?"

"We are getting out of here."

Emma has heard Tim say those words many times before, but this time his tone tells her that he is no longer just hopeful, but that this time he is sure of it. "We are?" she says, trying to be optimistic.

Tim confidently states, "Five weeks, and all you have to do is be in your hut."

This sounds too good to be true. Emma shuts her eyes and ponders Tim's words. "That's splendid, Tim."

Tim frowns and taps on the wall. "Aye... don't you trust me?"

Emma remembers all the times he has asked those words and how every time he has never let her down. She answers, "With all my heart."

The two try to stay up together, but they soon both fall asleep. Abruptly the doors of Tim's hut swing open as the captives file in after a long day's work. Their chains clink with every step. As they huddle inside, the soldiers remove their cuffs and depart, leaving the men cold and desolate.

Not a single man enters the walls. They all stare at the beaten one kneeling in a heap. Several come over to Tim and help to lift him into his shelf. Watching in silence, all heads turn as Tim's attacker from the night before rushes to the front of the group. He reaches out and presents to Tim the thin dirty pillow from his own shelf. He places the hardened piece of leather, split and cracked, under Tim's head with the same hands that had been around his neck.

He then takes Tim's shoulders and apologizes

to him in German. All Tim can do is smile back. The audience slowly begins to siphon off to their shelves, except for Rupert.

"You Americans crazy," Rupert says with teary eyes.

Tim looks at his friend. "Sometimes you have to do what is good... even if it is crazy." Rupert laughs and mutters as he climbs into his shelf, "Honorable, respectful."

"Tim?" Emma's voice comes through the hole.

Tim responds, "We should rest. Work hard tomorrow, it will be one of the last days you see this place."

Emma opens her mouth, but then stops. Tim does not need to know of her plan, she thinks.

CHAPTER EIGHTEEN

Emma enters the black building eagerly. Helena has worked her first kitchen shift. When the Nazis unshackle Emma, she looks around immediately for Johanna. When she spots her, Emma walks over to an adjacent sewing wheel. Women occupy both of the wheels next to Johanna, so Emma chooses one in the row directly behind her.

"*Psst*," Emma whispers to Johanna the moment she sits at her sewing table. Johanna does not turn. "*Psst*, Johanna!" she tries again.

This time Johanna turns.

"Johanna, what did your sister find out? What did she see?"

"Nothing."

"She saw something, Johanna. She saw a new path in the black building. She saw doors, hallways, she saw new things. What did she see that we can use?" Emma persists.

"I asked her. Happy? I asked her, and she let me know she did not find out a thing. No new things came from her leaving here! I wish she was still sewing next to me."

"I am sorry your sister is not here with you anymore, but it is for the better. You must see that," Emma tries to console her, but Johanna turns silently back to her sewing wheel.

"Johanna," Emma whispers again, but she continues to work without turning around.

"Johanna!" Emma whispers once more, but this time even louder. "Why in the blazes did you not leave a wheel open for me next to you? It is dangerous to talk like this."

"They were here when I sat," Johanna replies without turning around.

"Ugh," Emma plops her face into some fabric. Lifting her head again, she sees that it is an officer's patch. She traces her thumb over the patch's grooves before looking around for a soldier.

"Hauptleute... Hauptleute!" Emma calls out. She makes eye contact with a soldier and again cries, "Hauptleute!"

The soldier rushes over to her but slows when he makes out what Emma is saying. He appears puzzled and turns to another soldier. The two exchange a few words before one of them steps out of the room. Within a minute the soldier comes back, following Marcel, who approaches Emma, but before he reaches her, he commands the soldier to walk away.

When Marcel reaches Emma, he clears his throat but remains silent. He stands beside her waiting for her to speak.

"Marcel, I..."

"Hauptleute," he interrupts.

"Hauptleute, I am most cold here... with the machines. My hands have grown sore, too, see?" Emma raises her hands palms-up. "Is there a way we could go back to your room again, where it is warm?"

Marcel looks around and then extends his hand. Emma floats her hand down into his palm and allows him to raise her from her stool. Johanna peers over her shoulder and watches.

Marcel escorts Emma from the needlework room and back to his quarters. After leaving the factory, but before the two make it much farther than that, she slows her pace drastically at the sight of a hallway and asks, "What's down there?"

Pausing mid-step, Marcel turns around with his hands clasped behind him and strolls back to where Emma has stopped. He peers down the hallway. "That, dear, is where our radio men work. There are radio stations in both rooms at the end there." He smiles and turns with the expectation that Emma will continue to follow.

"But surely not every door down there is for radio. There are many doors," Emma says.

Marcel makes a quizzical face. He walks back to Emma and looks down the hallway again. "Yes, you are correct. The two rooms at the end are for radio communication as I mentioned and the other three I believe are just for equipment storage."

"What kind of equipment?" Emma asks.

Marcel narrows his eyes. Emma knows she

walks a thin line but continues to wait for an answer. Marcel smiles, raises his eyebrows and extends his hand, allowing Emma to lead the way down the hall. Marcel opens the first door they come to so she may look inside.

The room houses two grimy buckets, a broom, and two mops with heads that have turned brown from use. Marcel shuts the door and walks to the next. It is just an empty room with tile flooring, though bigger than the utility closet she saw before.

Finally, they walk to the third door. This room is quite big, bigger than the utility closet and the barren room combined. Corrugated fiberboard storage boxes fill it from front to back and nearly reach the ceiling. A pathway exists from the door to the back wall for one to make his or her way down the room. It smells of rich cheese and bread.

Marcel steps inside and allows Emma all the time she wants to look around while he keeps one leg out in the hallway and one hand on the doorknob. Emma steps inside and looks all around. Marcel grins. "Satisfied?"

Emma says nothing as she marches out of the room and back into the hallway. Marcel's face twists a bit as he shuts the door. "Are we ready to walk now?" he asks.

Emma nods at Marcel, and he leads the way back to his room. Along the way Emma sees another hallway with two doors. This one extends about twenty yards before turning left to form another hallway. She sees a total of five hallways on her trip with

Marcel.

Emma whispers to herself, "How do I find it?"

Marcel and Emma reach his quarters, and he stops to pull out the room key. Emma takes a long look around. As she does, Marcel looks over his shoulder at her. The two enter the room. Marcel pockets his keys, walks around his desk, and puts his hands under the side flaps of his officer's coat.

Emma walks almost to the middle of the room. She grips her gown with both hands and looks down at her feet. Marcel narrows his eyes and tilts his head. "What, my dear?"

Emma looks up with wide eyes and shakes her head.

"My dear, you have been awfully peculiar. What's in your mind?"

Emma walks towards the window and looks out. "I am curious about this place."

Marcel smiles. "Well yes, that can be seen very well. What about this place makes you curious?" He steps around his desk to come closer to her.

"Just curious."

Marcel raises his eyebrows, lets out a sigh. "Well, um, the building, it is old. It was at first a prison, but I turned it into much more, and..."

Emma interrupts, "What about that?"

He steps forward and looks in the direction she is pointing.

"Ah, my masterpiece, the Raupe," Marcel boasts in a showman's voice. "I never gave it a name, but my men here chose that and, well, to be sincere, I like it. I am certain you must have heard of it by now."

"I have," Emma responds.

He smiles and looks at her. "I wanted something large and daunting, yet simple. I think I achieved that."

"Why make anything at all?" Emma asks. "Bullets kill us all the same."

"No, no, no, my dear—bullets do not have the vitality that my creation does, and it is the vitality of the Raupe that men fear the most!"

"No one fears your Raupe, bullets would work the same," Emma remarks with disdain.

Marcel's muscles tighten but then relax before he responds. "My dear, if you try to get under my skin, you have found the right conversation, but I can see through your lies. My Raupe stirs fear into every heart and soul on this island, including my men. Bullets don't keep order as well as it does."

"And why is that?"

"You have a tongue today?" Marcel chuckles. "This is why, my dear." He opens a cabinet door underneath his desk and pulls out a metal can. He puts it on his desk and places a pointed finger down on top of it. The can is stubby, rising as high off the desk as a clenched fist.

"This is the magic that makes my creation so special." Marcel's voice quivers with excitement. Emma's eyes widen as she gulps hard.

"This is the last thing that all the Raupe's victims taste before they die. This corrodes them from the inside out." Marcel brings his hand from his mouth down to his chest and then to his stomach, with curled fingers.

A tear slips down the side of Emma's nose. "Why?"

"Because that is what my mind does, dear. It's genius."

"But...why?"

Marcel looks down at his desk and smiles. "Jews do not deserve to die the way men do, by a bullet. They should suffer like the vermin they are. Like pests, bacteria, they are an infection wherever their presence exists."

He looks at Emma with piercing eyes. Blood rushes to his face as he says with a laugh, "I am the ungeziefer jäger... their exterminator."

When Marcel flushes red, Emma notices the scar on his neck. Her hand involuntarily rises to her own throat and she asks, "You... you have been in it, haven't you?"

"What?"

"Your neck... it is scarred. I have heard that the Raupe clamps about your neck, like the jaws of a lion..."

Marcel steps further behind his desk, away from Emma. "Love gave me this scar."

Emma remains quiet.

"My wife—she let me call her my wife—was with another." As he speaks, he flexes his fingers like the prongs of a fork. Pressing his digits into the desk until they are white, he continues. "She was beautiful, the Jew, I saw instantly why my wife picked her."

He takes a step around his desk towards her, as she backs away from him. They are slowly circling his desk.

Marcel says, "I wanted them both... and I wanted to hurt them, at once; I didn't know what I wanted."

Emma, now brushing against Marcel's desk, grazes her hand over the tin can. Marcel says, "I locked the door behind me and lunged for them. I did not know what I was doing, but they did. It was as if they had planned for me to surprise them." He takes another step towards her. "They attacked me. They pinned me in those ghastly sheets, and my wife grabbed the hunting knife she inherited from her grandfather."

Emma takes a step around the desk, further from Marcel. She grabs the tin can without lifting it up. Marcel raises his hands and says with tears and a smile, "I haven't touched a knife since."

Tears swell in Emma's eyes and she whispers, "You... you should have died."

Marcel, frozen with his hands still in the air, lets Emma's words burn for a moment. He reaches to grab his stallion paperweight and hurls it at her.

Emma ducks her head just in time to avoid getting hit. The brass weight crashes through a wooden panel on his cabinet, disappearing through a massive hole. As she rises back up, she hoists the tin can behind her head. She shakes but does not throw it.

Marcel stares at Emma, then quickly walks towards her. She shouts, "Stay back!" She is unable to release the can.

He grabs her wrists and shakes her aggressively. She drops the can, but when she does, his eyes widen. With quick reflexes he catches it before it hits the ground. Emma breaks free and runs to the other side of the room, by the door. She turns in fright but sees Marcel sit in his desk chair.

"I want to go back now, please... let me go back now," Emma says.

Marcel inhales deeply and closes his eyes. He opens them again and looks at the can in his hands, then at Emma, then back at the can, before replacing it in the cabinet under his desk. He stands, chuckles, and walks towards Emma in a slow, benign manner.

Emma stands petrified against the door.

He takes her hands in his. "You need not worry. I would never put you in it, my dear, not you."

"Please, I want to go back now," Emma asks again as tears trail down her cheeks.

Marcel lets go of her hands and walks back to his chair. "Take off your clothes," he says, from behind his desk.

Emma stands still and stares at him with a stern expression.

Marcel leans back in his chair. "I am waiting."

Emma slowly begins to shake all over. Her eyes stay focused on Marcel.

"Take off your clothes... now," Marcel commands.

Tears course down Emma's face. Marcel pulls out the metal can again and places it on the desk before sliding it slightly forward in Emma's direction.

Emma releases a gasping laugh and shakes her head. "I will not."

Marcel taps his armrest with one finger and then pounds the top of his desk hard. He walks to Emma and places one hand around her throat, under her jaw, and grabs her right wrist with his other hand. He inhales aggressively while staring at her. He slides her across the wall until they reach the foot of his bed, knocking an empty coat rack to the floor.

Emma's face flushes, but she does not take her eyes off Marcel. In one motion he lets her go and turns around. He knocks the metal can onto its side with the back of his hand. He curls his fingers like a gorilla and leans forward on his desk, placing pressure on his knuckles.

"Get out!" Marcel commands.

Emma does not hesitate. She runs to the door and exits.

CHAPTER NINETEEN

Safe outside Marcel's room, Emma falls to the ground. The soldiers on guard outside grab her by the arms. In response to Marcel's shouted command, the soldiers drag Emma to her feet and down the hall, back to her sewing machine.

Johanna watches Emma as the soldiers bring her back and throw her into her sewing chair. She turns around and whispers, "Well?"

Emma leans her elbows on her thighs and looks down. She sniffles and wipes her eyes with a soft sock before finding the courage to load her spindle with thread and go back to work.

"Well?" Johanna whispers again, louder this time.

"Well, what?"

"Did you do it?"

Emma squints and drops her hands to her sewing table. "Are you ossified? Of course I didn't do it."

Johanna frowns and scrunches up her shoulders. "I thought that was why you went to see him."

"No, I went to see him to find out where the... listen, we must sit together tomorrow. I will not talk to you until then."

Johanna says nothing.

Emma looks down at the black thread in her machine and pulls some slack out with her index finger. She continues to tug until much of the thread is loose. She twirls her finger in the thread one time, two times, three times, again and again, until the end of her finger turns purple.

She unravels her finger from the thread, wraps it back up, grabs the little wooden cylinder, and drops it into her tattered blouse.

A soldier with grey wool gloves tucked under his belt has been observing Emma since she sat down. He stands too far away from Johanna and Emma to hear them speak, but he sees what she does with the black thread.

The day continues. Sew, sew, bread and water, sew, urinate and defecate in the pit outside, sew, sew some more, watch the sun lower, sew and sew. When the day reaches its end, a soldier's loud shout halts all the working women.

The captives silently stand and line up in front of their machines. They stare at the back of each other's heads with their wrists and ankles close together for binding.

After the soldiers chain the women, they escort the lines out of the black building. Before reaching the last door to the outside, two soldiers stop the line. Emma is close to the back of the first line, so she tries to peek around the woman in front of her to see why they do not move.

A soldier wearing grey wool gloves walks down the line of women. He steps past a few, checking their faces. He returns to observe one woman's face a moment longer, but then continues walking and checking. When he reaches Emma, he smiles, points to her and calls for another soldier to come. The grey-gloved Nazi points to Emma's wrists, and the other soldier unlocks her hands and feet. Gloved hands grab her by the forearm and aggressively tug her to the side.

"Wait!" Emma cries.

She pulls back, but the hands are too strong. She stumbles across the floor, trying to keep up with the Nazi tugging her into a corner.

Squeezing Emma's arm tightly, cutting off the circulation to her fingers, the Nazi shouts in German, "Carry on."

The door to the outside opens. It is a quiet evening. No wind or snow rushes in, only a red-orange glow as the women exit the building. A pair of soldiers take interest in Emma and the gloved Nazi, and they walk over.

"Please," Emma says.

"'Please,' it says. You speak English. Interesting, I think. I like English," the Nazi says, as he takes off the glove on his right hand.

Emma glares at him. "Do not touch me!"

"Shh, shhh," the Nazi says with one finger pressed to his lips. "You have something that belongs to me." The other two soldiers stand behind him.

Emma looks down. Sweat moistens her palms. Her legs shake when the brisk air hits her as the last line of women leave.

With his finger, the Nazi prods Emma's navel through her tattered shirt. She flinches but remains still. He probes again, but a little higher, and when he does, the spindle caught in Emma's undergarment moves. He smiles and pushes his hand up her shirt, sliding the spindle out of her collar.

The Nazi catches the thread as it falls. When the spindle plops into his hand, the soldiers behind him chuckle.

"Is this yours?" the Nazi asks.

A tear slips down Emma's cheek. Her lips quiver slightly. She nods but doesn't break eye contact.

"This does not belong to..." the Nazi says, pointing his finger at Emma's face. With his hand so close to her face she can feel the warmth of his skin. She continues to stare into his eyes.

"Hmpf," the Nazi says. He holds the spindle up and fiddles with it between his fingers, breaking eye contact with Emma to look at the soft wood. He looks at her again. "Did you steal from me, Jew?"

Emma shuts her eyes and raises her hands behind her head. The soldiers all watch. With a few quick strokes she pulls her hair into a bun. She extends her hand out, palm up. The Nazi sets the spindle in Emma's palm, expressionless. She unravels some thread from the spindle with one hand while holding her hair back with the other. After she gets enough thread from the spindle, Emma reaches behind her head and wraps it around her bun four times. When she finishes, she snaps the string. Her hair stays in place.

The Nazi takes the spindle from her and smiles as he looks at the other soldiers. He laughs, then reaches for Emma's collar. He pulls it down further than necessary and drops the spindle inside. He steps forward until he is shoulder to shoulder with her and looks down at Emma... she does not look back.

"Shh," the Nazi says with a grin, before walking away.

The two remaining soldiers grab Emma by the wrists and pull her to the end of the hall, outside, and all the way to her hut, where she runs to her shelf and slides inside.

E is resting in her shelf with her eyes closed when Emma runs by. She opens her eyes briefly but goes back to resting after Emma passes. "You are well?" she asks with closed eyes.

"Yes, E," Emma says.

On her back, Emma takes out the spool of thread. She unravels the string until she has enough to measure the length of her forearm at least ten times, then twists it into a stubby rope. With her thickened string in hand, Emma squeezes each end and pulls it taut against her throat.

The smooth rope catches under her chin. Her face reddens, but only slightly. She lets out a brief cough, then presses her knees against the bottom of the shelf above her and pulls tighter.

Fatigue loosens the muscles in Emma's shoulders and arms. The tangled thread unravels. She breathes heavily. Her heart pounds hard, more from the exertion than from choking.

Emma looks out from her shelf, sees that no one takes notice of her, and places her hands across her face. Holding back tears, she thinks in silence.

She tries again, pulling the tiny rope as hard as her muscles will allow, but she is still able to breathe without much difficulty. After a minute, she releases and relaxes again.

If it won't work on my neck, it won't work on his.

As her chest expands and contracts, tears run down her cheek. Emma slaps the brick wall next to her, then her wooden shelf. Sharp pain pierces her palm, and she jerks her hand back. Looking down, she sees blood dripping down her pale forearm.

Emma inspects the inner edge of her shelf. She sees the splintered crack she made the night Ackerman confronted her. The jagged wood protrudes in every direction. She squeezes her dress a bit with her cut hand to staunch the bleeding, and picks at the crack. She picks and pulls and twists a spur of wood until breaks loose.

Emma brings the wood to the edge of her shelf and looks at it. It is a sturdy piece, but she notices a perfectly round hole that disrupts its integrity. She reaches back down to the split in her shelf. She searches with her fingers until she locates what she hoped to find. She pulls and pulls, eventually loosening it from its position. She pulls it up to her face. It is a nail, which matches the size of the hole in the splinter.

Emma fits the head of the nail into a curved groove at the end of the broken piece. With its pointed tip protruding straight up, and a groove pinching it in place, Emma begins to bind the nail to the wood with her thread.

One wrap, two wraps, five wraps, fifteen wraps, thirty wraps, and the nail is secure. Emma presses down on the tip of the nail, finding that it resists without budging or wiggling. She stabs her shank into her shelf. The nail sticks in the wood, forcing her to tug it loose.

"Mausebär, what are you doing?" E asks. "You have been making much noise."

Emma hides her shank in the crack of the shelf. "I am just moving, trying to get myself comfortable."

"You are bleeding," E says when Emma slides out, revealing the dried blood on her arm.

"Oh, goodness, yes! Odd how we can hurt ourselves and never notice until later," she replies.

E shakes her head and tugs on Emma's shirt, gesturing for her to sit on the ground. She sits, and E joins her. "Let me have a look. You cut your hand? How do you not notice a cut hand, Mausebär?"

Emma pulls her hand away. "I don't know. I get cuts a lot around here. Maybe I am just getting used to it." She stands and turns away from E.

"I worry about you," E says, placing her hand softly upon Emma's shoulder. "You have been distant."

Emma's body relaxes, but she remains turned away.

"And I hear of your visits to the Hauptleute," E says.

Emma tenses and turns around, letting E's hand fall away. "You don't know what I am doing. Stop looking over me. Why won't you just trust me?" Tears well up in her eyes. E stares softly at her and then embraces her.

"Very well, Mausebär, very well... I will trust you."

CHAPTER TWENTY

Each day, Marcel orders that Tim be allowed to rest, but that he is still supposed to tally at the end of the week. His mercy apparently has limits. Udo and Tim go straight to work; they enjoy each other's company now. As the two commence their duties, Tim tries again to talk to his new friend, but this time in German.

Tim holds up a rifle to Udo and says, "Gewehr?"

Udo looks at him curiously as Tim tries to say the word for gun. He tries again, this time working even harder to mimic an authentic German accent.

Udo repeats the word slowly, correcting the misplaced accent. Tim repeats the word but slightly better. Udo nods with a smile and continues to work.

Tim grins proudly and holds up his pencil. "Bleistift?"

Udo nods in approval. He is impressed; Tim has pronounced the word for pencil flawlessly. He decides to play along, so he points to his face. "Aye?"

Tim is delighted to have Udo inquire about his language but is confused at what he is trying to say. He motions for the man to repeat himself. This time Udo points directly to his eyeball. Tim laughs. "Oh, eye."

Udo parrots "eye" back to Tim and smiles when the American nods.

Decades and language separate the two men, yet they interact with each other like close friends. They go back and forth for hours, learning new words; Tim laughs hard, but under his breath so as not to alert the guards. After a while they both agree they should go back to work, lest they forget about the task at hand for the whole night.

Tim looks at Udo after he marks his last unit for the night and asks, "Erledigt?" which means "Finished?"

Udo holds up a finger, and says in English with a strong German accent, "One more."

Tim smiles and walks over to place his clipboard on the table by the door, but something catches his attention. He scans the top sheet and examines the tallies, noticing a pattern. On each column, under Rupert's serial number, there is an obviously disproportionate amount of failed weapons for each station he has worked for the past week. Tim looks at the second sheet and finds the same pattern there. Eyes narrowing, Tim moves back to the table where he started for the night while tracing his finger down his paper to one of the weapons he examined. He checks the tag number on the document, finds the gun that matches the tag number, and pulls its trigger.

The trigger does not move back into place. It is so loose that it is nearly independent from the gun itself. Tim tries to remain calm as he scrolls down the sheet and finds another gun that he marked unsatisfactory. When he pulls its trigger, he finds that it suffers from the same deficiency as the other, only this time the trigger is so loose that it falls out of the gun entirely and hits the floor with a *tink*.

Tim looks at a pistol which failed to pass, on which the trigger also wobbles too loose for use. He continues down the list faster and faster, and finds that nearly all of the faulty guns have malfunctioning triggers.

Udo watches Tim anxiously reexamine the weapons and walks over to see what the problem could be. As he approaches, Tim looks at Udo's clipboard—holding them side by side, he sees that it has the same patter. The guns Udo marked unsatisfactory have loose triggers as well. Tim slams the clipboards on the table and yells, "Rupert... idiot!"

The soldiers outside hear Tim shout and open the door. Udo asks them for just a little more time to finish. The soldiers are suspicious but close the door. Tim looks at Udo. "We must change these."

Udo stares at Tim, confused.

"We must change these!" he repeats and begins erasing his top sheet of paper.

Udo grabs Tim's clipboard away and looks at him as if he has gone insane. He speaks, but Tim can't understand the rapid German. He grabs for the clipboard but misses as Udo snatches his own clipboard, too, and runs away. Tim tackles him to the ground, wrestling for the papers.

The guards hear the commotion and run in to break up the scuffle. Once Tim and Udo are separated, the guards start bashing them both with their guns. Tim looks up to see Udo shielding himself with his old frail arms. The next instant, the old man is brutally struck with a rifle butt. Tim throws himself on top of Udo to protect him as the two soldiers continue to beat them both.

Tim clenches his jaw under the agonizing blows. He squeezes Udo tightly. Soon the soldiers stop and then cuff Tim. When they move to cuff Udo, however, he isn't moving. Tim's eyes water as he sees Udo's cracked skull on the smooth concrete floor. He cries out, "No!"

One of the Nazis kicks the motionless body to see if he is dead. He is.

Tim is speechless.

The soldier shrugs and begins to move Tim out of the room. Tim erupts, thrashing and screaming until he rips free and falls on Udo's body. "Udo! Udo!" he cries frantically. Tears roll down Tim's cheeks and off his chin, falling onto Udo's gaunt, grey face.

The soldiers pull Tim up, but he fights his way back down again. One of the soldiers bashes the back of his head twice with a rifle. He loses consciousness for a moment, then recovers, but the strength to keep fighting is knocked from him.

As the soldiers drag him from the room, they decide that, rather than return him to his hut, it will be best to take him somewhere else first. Across the island and into the big black building, Tim finds himself in front of a door.

His dripping face splatters sweat and blood

down towards his feet as the soldiers knock on the door. After a moment Marcel stands in the doorway, wearing a simple white shirt and blue pants. The soldiers explain what has happened and hand him the two clipboards stained with blood.

Marcel orders them to bring Tim in and then to wait in the hall. Tim sits down in the chair facing the desk. Marcel goes behind his desk and leans over it. He asks, "Are you a religious man, American?"

Tim says nothing.

Marcel asks, "Did you hear me?"

"I am," Tim responds.

"Then tell me this: do you believe God put you here and desires you alive, and it is the devil who is trying to kill you," Marcel asks with a grin. "Or do you believe the devil dragged you here and is trying to kill you, but God is trying to get you out of here alive?"

Tim lowers his head. "I'm not familiar with what God desires."

Marcel slouches into his own seat.

"Would it matter?" Tim adds.

"Which team always matters," Marcel responds. He pauses before changing the subject. "My men say you were attacked. They ran in and found that your attacker was trying to ruin your documentation and that you tried to stop him. Why was he trying to destroy your paperwork?"

"I don't know."

Marcel nods. "I see... how could you know? He did not speak your language. So, the way my men described it... that is what happened?"

Tim wants to tell the true story and honor Udo, but he thinks of Emma and simply nods. Marcel stands up and walks to the window, looking out into the night.

"It must be cold in those huts... but, of course, a place like that is fitting for a Jew, wouldn't you say?"

"I am not Jewish," Tim responds.

Marcel spins around. "I am sorry, what was it you said?"

"I am not a Jew."

"Yes, well you have been living with them long enough now, you might as well consider yourself to be. After all, plagues do spread."

"Is that what you consider these people... a plague?"

"Well, of course. Anathemas mating and reproducing I believe, is a disease, a disease which has plagued Germany and the world since Christ."

"And how do you come to that conclusion?" Tim asks.

Marcel pulls a cigar and matches from a drawer. He carefully cuts off its end with a guillotine-like clip. "You really need to speak to my successor."

"I hope to do so."

Marcel lights a match and holds it burning in the air. "One day the entire world will have that pleasure... because one day, the whole world will be his."

Tim looks at Marcel. "If *his* world will be anything like *your* island, then there may actually be someone out there more charming than you."

Marcel throws his head back and laughs. Still

chuckling, he holds the match to the end of his cigar and takes several short puffs. "That is a good one, American! That is a good one."

Tim imagines shoving the burning cigar down Marcel's throat. The Nazi drops an ash into the ashtray. Marcel's face grows hard. "How is your wife, Miss Emmeline?"

Tim fights to keep from showing any emotion. He doesn't answer.

"On my island, American, the walls tell their secrets."

After a few more puffs Marcel stands up, a vile smile spreading across his lips.

Tim stiffens. "If you touch her... I swear to God, if you touch her, I..."

Marcel interrupts. "What makes you so sure I haven't already?"

Tim's mouth opens in dread then closes tightly.

"Tell me something, how is that you were beaten by an old half-Jewish man?" As Marcel finishes his question, he lunges forward, grabs Tim's left wrist, and grinds the cigar into his skin.

The pain almost throws Tim into shock. Marcel's smile widens. His dark eyes watch Tim writhe in agony. Tim restrains himself as long as he can before he shoves Marcel away and falls to the floor. The Nazi returns to his chair and relights his cigar, calling for his men to take Tim back to his hut. As they do Marcel laughs, "Until I see you again, American."

Tim holds his forearm as the soldiers drag him outside. Stepping into the cold, he sees that the soldiers have prepared a bonfire. *The Raupe is going to eat tonight*, he thinks. When they arrive at the hut, the soldiers throw Tim to the ground. They shut the door behind him, leaving him in darkness. He crawls to his shelf and slides inside, defeated. He squeezes his arm before slumping onto the thin wood.

Tim pulls the reed he has kept hidden from a small crevice in the wall and twirls it for a moment. The image of Marcel puffing his cigar is vivid in his mind as he sticks an end of the reed in his mouth to chew. When he does, he feels a sensation on his tongue from the blade—cool air. He puffs through the grass again to see if it was just his imagination, and to his surprise, he finds that the reed is hollow.

Half an hour later, the door flies open, letting moist, grey air fill the shelves. Three soldiers with lanterns barge in and begin to pull captives' shirts up over their chests. They examine each serial number until they reach the back of the hut. Tim closes his eyes as a tear seeps out.

"I am so sorry, Rupert," Tim whispers.

A Nazi tugs Rupert's shirt up and yells for the other two. A black bag is thrown over Rupert's head and the Nazis drag him out of his shelf and down the aisle while he screams in German, in English, and in every other language he knows. Tim gets out of his shelf and follows behind, trying to chase after him, to save him. His vision becomes blurred except for the sight of his kicking friend and the grey-uniformed soldiers who drag him away.

When the metal door shuts and locks again

Tim slams his body against it, fixing his eye through the square hole. He watches as the soldiers take Rupert away. Tim pounds his fists against the door and screams with rage. When he does, a few chips of rusted metal fall from the hinges.

Tim slams his back against the door and slides down to the floor weeping. He wants to save his friend, but he can't; he wants to honor his death by witnessing him go, but he can't force himself to watch. Screams from the outside pierce the hearts of everyone in the hut. All the men watch as Tim sobs, and some add tears of their own. Not one gives a disapproving glance. They let him purge his sorrow and mourn silently with him. Tim finally drops his limp hands to the floor and curls his legs small. His jaw hangs open, allowing the still hut air to flow inside.

CHAPTER TWENTY-ONE

Emma enters the factory. Out of routine she walks her way to a sewing machine next to Johanna.

Silence builds between them until Emma asks, "How are you?"

Without looking over, Johanna replies, "Quite fine, and you?"

Emma surveys the room for watchful eyes before reaching for Johanna's hand and revealing the shank hidden beneath her blouse.

"What is that?" Johanna whispers.

"It is a tool. I am going to use it on Marcel," Emma says, still surveying the factory.

"How?"

Emma threads her sewing machine. "Don't mind yourself with that. I will make it happen."

"Very well, and what then?"

"What do you mean, what then?" Emma focuses on the fabric she is mending. "Then the ruler of this island will be gone."

"Yes, and what then? You do not understand the

Nazis. They will replace him, again, and again." Johanna says.

"No, you do not understand. With Marcel gone, I will be alone. I will have his office, his radio, his phone, I will send for help."

Johanna grabs a pair of sleeping trousers, whips them through the air to remove wrinkles, then slides them across her machine for inspection. "It won't work."

"I believe it will. I believe your sister would agree."

Johanna's lips press hard together as she folds the finished pair of trousers.

Emma goes back to sewing as well. After a moment, she looks at Johanna, then raises her hand and calls for a soldier.

Johanna makes a small scoffing sound.

As the soldier comes near, Emma says, "Hauptleute, the Hauptleute, danke."

The soldier approaches her at a brisk pace. Emma smiles cordially, waiting for him to turn and fulfill her request, but he keeps walking. Her smile fades. When he reaches Emma, he grabs her right hand, slams it onto the table, and then screams at her in German. The Nazi turns around again, leaving her holding her wrist while fighting back tears.

"Looks as if the Hauptleute has forgotten about you," Johanna says.

Emma looks at Johanna with disdain and then stares in confusion at the soldier who hurt her.

CHAPTER
TWENTY-TWO

The next morning is bitter. Tim stumbles to take his place in line as the Nazis scream orders. For the first time, he doesn't see the back of Rupert's head. The men are shackled together and marched into the factory. He takes his seat and looks to where Rupert would have worked; another man has taken his spot. Tim has felt so much pain during his time on the island that he thinks there isn't any pain left to feel, yet he still hurts when he remembers his lost friends. Tim works his shift in a lifeless stupor. Even the thought of Emma doesn't soothe his ache.

As he goes through the motions of his duty, he hears a voice directly behind him, barely a whisper. "Don't turn around," the voice says.

Tim can feel breath on the back of his neck. He is alarmed but stays facing forward. The voice continues, "If you are able to escape this island, there will be a boat on the mainland, directly south near the harbor. I'm unaware of its docking times, but I can tell you that it only shows up at night, and it is there to help."

Tim keeps his eyes on his work as the voice says, "The Swedish government has learned of the formal coup d'état of the Nazis here in Germany. They know things are amiss. The boat is from them, for citizens who want to evacuate Germany without going through customs. It has a beacon, a flashing blue light. It signals that the boat is harbored but will be departing soon back to Sweden. If you escape this place, and are lucky enough, you can catch it."

Tim is frozen in place. No more words are spoken. After several moments he finds the nerve to turn around and sees that whoever was behind him is gone. He looks around the room. In the corner of the factory Tim makes eye contact with the one-eyed man, who nods in his direction. No one else acts as if anything unusual has happened. He goes back to work but instead of feeling despondent, he works with a bit of energy.

That night, when he enters his hut and crawls into his shelf, he hears Emma's soft whisper through the wall.

Tim presses his mouth against the hole in the wall. "Hello, Beautiful, how are you doing?"

Emma answers, "I am fair. How are you?"

"I have some miraculous news."

"What is it?"

"Well, it's only so certain, but there is a good chance we will have a chauffeur waiting to take us out of Germany when we get out of here."

Emma laughs and teases, "Oh, really now?"

Tim whispers, "Yes."

"You still haven't told me how you plan to get us out," Emma says.

"Let me worry about that. You remember what I told you, right?"

"Yes, I remember. I will be in my shelf waiting."

Tim smiles and leans back. The one-eyed man looks at him sideways. "I hope you are successful, American. If any of us deserve to leave this place, it is you."

"Thank you," Tim closes his eyes.

Emma yawns and whispers, "Good night" through the hole and then shuts her eyes as well.

Tim breathes deeply and smiles. He stares at the bottom of Rupert's shelf, which is now occupied by another captive. "Four weeks left."

Another week passes, and Tim watches a pile of firewood slowly grow larger. The men see the pile before entering the dark building, and they all think the same thing: *Raupe.*

Another fifteen hours of labor come to a close and one more day is over. Tim is lying in his shelf. He notices that the days are getting shorter and shorter as his dream of freedom grows more and more vivid. Tim falls asleep thinking about home and the first things he will do once he gets there, all of which involve Emma. Fresh tears run down his cheeks as he realizes that for the first time since he came to the island, he is completely fearless. He is ready to escape.

CHAPTER
TWENTY-THREE

The hut door opens. Emma is already awake. She has not tried to reach Marcel again since her hand was slammed against her sewing table. She still talks with Johanna, but only small talk, if any at all.

"Emma…" E says.

Emma lies in her shelf. All the other women line up in the hut, except for her. As the Nazis walk through, cuffing the women to one another, another woman with dark hair, a few shelves closer to the door than Emma, also remains in her shelf.

Emma turns her head and slides to better see the woman through the line of captives. One uniform eventually makes his way to the woman's shelf. When he notices her, he slows his approach, and smiles. The man steps quieter, and quieter, as if he is approaching a small animal he does not want to startle. He grabs the woman by her hair and drags her onto the ground. Every captive in line stares at her own feet, not wanting to call attention to herself and not wanting to watch the fate of the woman with dark hair.

Emma can see that the woman is weak because she does not react when they stomp and kick her with their boots. The soldiers do not stomp her in a frenzy. They stomp as if to see if she is alive, though they stomp hard nonetheless. The woman lies on the ground, panting and bleeding. One soldier lifts her dress up, pretends to sniff, and pinches his nose with a sour look on his face. All the soldiers laugh.

The soldier who sniffed picks the woman up off the ground like a ragdoll and slings her light frame over his shoulder. He slaps her rump and winks at the other men.

"Psst... psst!" E tries frantically to attract Emma's attention.

"Dah!" a soldier shouts as he approaches E. When he reaches the back of the line, he sees Emma. He walks towards her, one hand on his pistol.

Emma smiles and reaches for her shank, tucked safely away in her hiding spot. When the soldier arrives, allowing the light from the door to shine more directly onto her face, he shouts to his comrades, one of whom joins him.

The soldiers talk.

Emma watches, waiting for one of them to make a quick move toward her, but instead, the first one takes his hand off his pistol and reaches out to her. He shouts aggressively but keeps his hand extended. The other soldier folds his arms and watches.

Emma looks over and sees E's forehead dripping with sweat. She lets go of her shank, takes the soldier's hand, and scoots out. The soldier walks her to the back of the line where he cuffs her hands and ankles.

Once all the Nazis are outside the hut, the line of women begins to move.

"Do you have a soldier?" E asks in a whisper.

"No, of course not."

"Mausebär, how could you do such a thing? Your husband still lives…"

"I do not have a solider. I would never do that." Emma remembers Ackerman's face.

"Then why would you not be harmed?" E asks.

Emma doesn't respond. She continues walking in the wake of E's disapproval.

CHAPTER TWENTY-FOUR

After another hard day's work, Emma and E are back in their hut. A soft orange glow falls across the entire island. E and Emma lie in their shelves. Neither of them speak. Silence looms between them as the other women occupy themselves.

Emma taps her shank with her fingers where it hides in the crack of her shelf.

Oddly, the front door opens.

The women in the hut become still. Never has the door swung open at such a time of day. The soldiers usually wait for all the female huts to be secure because that signifies that their work day is over and what the soldiers call "a good time" can begin.

The door opens all the same. The women do not panic because they do not know if they have a reason to panic. Two soldiers, dressed in formal military attire with coats, step into the hut. One stands by the open door while the other walks the length of the room. Emma, E, and all the other women watch as the Nazi walks straight through, paying no mind to any of the women.

As the soldier gets closer to Emma she reaches for her shank, only this time she brings it to her collar bone before tucking it down into her blouse. When the soldier reaches her, he says, "Emmeline Wexford, number 66611."

His English is rough, but Emma understands her own name. She slides out of her shelf and stands before the soldier.

"Come," he says.

Emma watches as he turns his back to her before walking away. She does not know what to do, so she follows. She feels the eyes of the women upon her, but she doesn't glance back at any of them. Once Emma and her escort leave the hut, the other soldier shuts and latches the door from the outside before accompanying them. Emma's two escorts walk towards the black brick building and she follows closely behind.

As she walks, Emma takes the liberty to look around a bit more than she usually does. The men in front of her appear to look straight forward, aside from an occasional glance at one another when either makes a comment in German. Looking across the island, she only notices the water. Everything appears to blur except for the sea.

She sees orange ripples trickling into one another under the sea breeze. The horizon seems to bend toward the sun, as if all the water falls off in the distance. Emma listens for waves sloshing against the island or for the low roar of currents off in the deep, but she hears neither. The water is silent. It makes no noise, but not for lack of having noise to make, not for lack of having a story to tell, but rather it is as if the waters hold a secret, only able to be heard by those willing to listen. Emma knows that to escape the island, it will have to be done through the water.

Having been lost in thought, Emma looks forward and sees the soldiers opening a door to the black building. They walk inside, and she follows. One of the soldiers flips a toggle to turn on the lights, but nothing happens. The black hall still shields sight from peering down its corridor. Pulling a flashlight from his belt, he flicks it on, sending a beam of light down the hallway. Emma shivers behind the Nazis in their wool coats.

She recognizes this part of the building and begins to sweat. Soon, the Nazis bring her to his door and knock upon it. Emma hangs her hands by her side but stands tall and leans forward. She notices dim light coming from under the door, as if it comes from a single lit candle.

When the door opens, Emma hears Marcel say, "Soldaten, gut gut." He stands in the doorway with a toothbrush in his mouth. He rubs his wet head with a beige towel, wearing his uniform pants with a white undershirt tucked in.

The two Nazis salute, then turn in step and walk back down the hallway. Marcel whisks his toothbrush back and forth in his mouth. In Emma's mind, the sound stirs the thought of what it once meant to be clean. Marcel smiles. He turns and sweeps his arm wide, inviting Emma inside. She sees a small flame glowing on Marcel's nightstand, fresh sheets, and a folded blue nightgown at the foot of the bed.

Marcel pulls the brush from his lips and sifts the pasty foam in his mouth with his tongue. "My dear, I have missed you."

He raises a finger and steps into his bathroom. Emma hears him spit into the sink. Marcel loudly gulps from a glass of water before swishing and spitting again.

She stands in the middle of the room waiting for Marcel to finish. When he returns, he approaches her with his toothbrush. White paste sits atop the soft bristles. A drop of water falls from the brush as he raises it to her mouth. "Go ahead."

Emma frowns and pulls her head back.

"Please, dear, I do not mind, you are not Jewish." Marcel raises the brush to Emma's lips.

She tucks her chin and turns her head. "Stop," she says, but Marcel does not stop. He continues to raise the brush until the paste touches her upper lip. He rubs the bristles between her lips until he finds bone. She wants to continue fighting him, but she does not. She unclenches her jaw and allows him to scrub the inside and outside of all her teeth. Marcel brushes slowly. He looks into her eyes while running his fingers through her hair.

After scrubbing every part in her mouth, Marcel stops and walks back to the bathroom sink to retrieve his glass. He fills it from a pitcher and hands it to Emma to sip and spit. She slurps, sloshes, then spits back into the glass. With the milky water in hand, Marcel runs back to his bathroom, empties the glass, and refills it. He returns, glass in hand, drinks from it, and places it on the corner of his desk. He folds his arms and smiles at Emma, who notices his anxious grin.

"Dear... will you stay here tonight with me?" Marcel asks.

"Is that a request? May I say no?"

Marcel replies, "My dear, I am offering you my bed, warmth, peace—you may stay here." He raises his hands in the air. "You do not have to wake tomorrow to work."

Emma examines Marcel's face. She crosses her arms over her belly. "You won't make me work in the morning?"

Marcel chuckles. "You won't work ever again, if you choose to lie in my bed."

She walks the length of his bed. Looking at the nightgown, she asks, "You want me to wear this?"

Marcel's eyes widen. He snatches the powder-blue gown up, squeezing it before extending it toward her. "Nothing would please me more."

She takes the gown and turns her back, unfolding the velvet garment and holding it by its shoulder straps. Marcel places his hands on her hips. Emma feels for her shank beneath her blouse and spins around, blocking Marcel with the gown between them. "May I have some privacy?" she asks.

Marcel steps back, his expression almost

blank except for a coy smile. "What do you need privacy for? I plan to see you nonetheless."

"If you want this lady, you must treat me like one."

He steps back and leans against his desk, gripping its edges. "You want to be alone?"

Emma, hiding her shank behind the nightgown, says, "I do."

Marcel crosses his arms and stares at her in silence. She stands still, shaking, but returning his gaze with equal firmness.

"We are the product of our choices," he says. "So, decide." He stands and walks to the door. "Knock when you are ready," he says, shutting it behind him as he leaves.

Emma waits a moment and then shakes until the shank falls to the floor. She hurriedly strips off her clothes and steps onto the nightgown puddled on the ground. She lifts it up her body and onto her shoulders but does not bother clasping it at the back. Instead, she grabs her shank from the ground and runs to Marcel's desk cabinet. She glances at the water making ripples in the glass at the corner of the desk.

Emma kneels and pulls the Zyklon-B can from the bottom cabinet. She pins the can to the wall with her knee, then raises her shank in the air. She stabs at the can several times, trying to be quiet, but barely makes a dent. She sticks her head above Marcel's desk and grabs the brass stallion paperweight, using it as a hammer to drive the nail through. One hit, and the lid is punctured.

Emma covers her mouth with one hand and carefully lifts the can. She thinks of the water glass, to pour the poison into it, to pour it down Marcel's throat, to pour a pathway back home. Anxious, excited, and thinking of Marcel's candlestick phone, she reaches for the water glass.

Suddenly, she freezes in place. Her jaw drops. She sees Marcel in the doorway... and he is not alone. Beside him stands a soldier wearing sleeping attire. A third person is between them. Emma feels she is about to drop the can, so she sets it on the desk. The three witnesses in the doorway say nothing. Marcel stares at Emma with hateful eyes, but she does not look at him. She stares at the woman between them. "Johanna."

Johanna does not look at Emma. She turns her face to the soldier by her side, reaches for his pocket and slides her hand inside. When Emma sees this, she snarls. "How could you? We were going to escape! You and your sister, all of us, we were going to escape!"

"You took Helena!" Johanna shouts.

Emma leaps for Johanna. She doesn't see Marcel or the other soldier, she doesn't see the room or the island or Tim, all she sees is Johanna's neck.

"No no, none of that, wretch!" Marcel says and grabs Emma in his arms."

Screaming, kicking, and thrashing with clawed hands, Emma tries to reach Johanna. Her soldier wraps a protective arm around her shoulders and ushers her into the hallway. Johanna shuts the door behind them.

Still screaming, Emma tries to escape Marcel's grip. He overpowers her, throwing her to the ground. She stands back up and lunges at Marcel, shank in hand. He steps to the side and pushes her over. She hits her head against the brick wall and everything goes dark.

CHAPTER TWENTY-FIVE

The next morning Emma opens her eyes. Blood has dried into a crust in her hair. The blue nightgown no longer adorns her body. Her old rags have been thrown over her. Emma hears whistling and remembers where she is. She rolls over, still in the corner of Marcel's room where she fell. Her neck cracks when she turns her head. The ground is hard, but nothing she isn't used to. Light barely peeks over the horizon through the window. She shivers and scoots toward the warmth beaming through the glass.

Marcel steps out of his bathroom, his uniform tight and his shoulders broad. Emma watches him as he moves about the room, putting pins in his coat pocket and brushing his hair to the side. "Ah, awake," he says when he sees her crawl across the floor. He walks to his bed and sits down.

"Did you make this?" Marcel asks, pulling out Emma's shank. She does not respond. "Fascinating," he says. "You would rather try to poison me than to try using this directly. I supposed it is a pitiful tool, you probably thought the same."

Emma, reaching the warm spot of sunlight, slips to the ground. She lies motionless, allowing the blood in her head to push out whatever it is that makes her cranium throb and her vision fuzzy.

Marcel grabs the wooden handle of the shank with both hands, straining to snap it in half. It remains in one piece. He sneers and drops it into a small metal trash can at the base of his desk, rubbing his hands together as one would do after a job well done.

Emma's eyes are closed, but she hears his boots approaching. She braces herself for a kick, but feels Marcel grab her by her hair and flip her onto her back. She opens her eyes and sees him standing over her. "I have found out what you love more than me, Emmeline, as I said I would. You will find it dead tonight. Think about your decisions more carefully; my patience has limits."

The room is spinning, and Emma's ears are ringing. Marcel walks out, leaving the door open. A Nazi walks in and hoists her up aggressively. She groans in anguish but manages to control her feet so that she walks as she is dragged along.

The Nazi takes Emma to the sewing factory, dumping her in the nearest chair. Her head lolls on her neck; she tries to fall asleep on the table, arms folded. The Nazi shouts and pulls Emma up by her hair.

She reaches for a saddle strap in the basket by her side, pulling it and straightening it under the machine. She pedals, but no thread comes out. She opens the machine and fills it with thread. A tear drips from the corner of her eye. She looks around her and sees all the other captives working with blank stares, mindlessly sticking pins into fabric and slowly dying. Johanna is gone.

Allowing her muscles to take her mind through the motions, Emma manages to work through the day. When the women hear the command, they all cease their work and stand in line. It has been hours since she was on the floor in Marcel's room, but she only now thinks about his last words to her: "I have found out what you love more than me... You will find it dead tonight."

She closes her eyes and weeps. She doesn't moan or fall to the floor, simply weeps. The tears are heavy and cling to her sooty cheeks, but Emma does not wipe them away. She doesn't mind the discomfort of the dirt clumping on her face. She pays no attention to her aches, her hunger, her thirst or desire for rest, she doesn't feel the new blisters on her ankles and wrists or the burn on her fingertips from having a dull needle that day—she only thinks of Tim.

The women march, and so does Emma. She stares at her feet, wanting the earth to split open and swallow her whole, wishing she could go back and never live, to go back to the beginning and keep her existence from ever happening, but she does exist, she does live, and her heart aches at the knowledge that Tim no longer does.

When she makes it back to her hut, she steps inside and waits for the Nazis to unshackle her. Before the cuffs come off, Emma looks down the line of women. She does not see E. She looks up and down the line, but E is nowhere in sight. When Emma's wrists are free, she walks in a hurry to the back of the hut, passing E's shelf, which is empty. She stands by her own shelf, griping her ragged clothes in balled fists, and waits for E to appear.

After the last woman's hands are freed, the Nazis leave, and the women move about in silence. A few captives begin to murmur, many others crawl into their shelves to rest, but E is not around to do either. Emma paces off the hut, examining each shelf, speeding up after each one reveals it does not house E. Making her way to the door, she turns around, shaking from head to foot. The women pay no attention.

Tears pour from Emma's eyes when she turns her head up to the roof of the hut. She lets out a long, loud groan. The women are silenced.

"No! He killed her!" Emma shouts.

She yells again and again, each time longer and louder than before. The women further from Emma put their heads down, while some of the women standing closer to her approach and embrace her. They hold her tightly and try to console her, they try to quiet her shouts, but Emma's voice can be heard halfway across the island.

She eventually falls to the floor and curls her knees to her chest. Other women weep next to her, because although she cannot express to them why she hurts, they feel her pain all the same.

The moon throws a blanket of night across the island from horizon to horizon. All the women have climbed into their shelves. Emma remains on the ground, eyes open but not focused on anything. Eventually she climbs to her feet. She stumbles to her shelf, inches her body inside, closes her eyes, and tries to fall asleep.

Within a moment, Emma hears the door of Tim's hut open. Another tear makes its way down her face but this time it streams its way to her smile.

"Hey, Beautiful, are you awake?"

"Yes, somehow, I am still here, Tim. I am still awake, and so are you."

"What is wrong?" Tim asks. "Your voice, you sound weak."

Emma fights back more tears. "E is gone... she is gone."

Tim searches his mind for the right words. After a pause, and listening to Emma sniffle through the wall, he says, "She had been here a long time, Emma. She is at peace now."

"It's my fault. I killed her," Emma whispers, tears still running down her face. "She watched over me. She was so kind, and I was so careless. I thought I could do this all on my own." Emma inhales deeply to slow her pounding heart. "But I can't."

Tim pats the wall. "Hey there, now stop. We are doing this, Emma, we are getting out."

"I trust you, believe me, I do, but you may be getting out of here without me, I am not strong enough to keep going," Emma says.

Tim leans back, collecting himself. "Stop. Don't say that. Don't think that, ever again. I made you a promise. I will get us out, I will get you out."

Emma's tears subside. "I trust you, Tim."

CHAPTER TWENTY-SIX

The next night Tim is just about to fall asleep when the metal door of Emma's hut bangs loudly. His eyes pop open and he hears the women screaming. Fear grips him, but he knows Emma will be safe once more. She has to be. He listens carefully. Wails and cries reverberate off the walls.

Through the screams Tim can faintly hear Emma coughing. After nearly sixty seconds of horror, all is silent. Tim is aware that he has been holding his breath and exhales slowly, then whispers, "Emma, are you alright?"

Silence. Nervousness grips his chest as he repeats his question. "Emma, are you all right?" His heart pounds, and he can feel the blood pulse through his head. "Emma!" he screams. There is no reply. "No!" Tim yells as he punches the wall.

He pushes out of his shelf and hits the ground with a thud. A hand reaches out and grabs him by the shirt. The one-eyed man grips him with bony fingers and asks in a raspy voice, "What are you doing? Remember your plan."

Tim slaps his hand away and shouts, "My plan doesn't involve my wife raped and murdered!" He gets up and runs to the metal door, grabbing the handle and yanking it violently, as if he has gone insane. The wet shirts hung on the hinges fall off. He jerks the handle again, yielding no more than a bit of squeaking and dust falling from the ceiling. Tim runs back to his shelf, clutches his thin pillow and returns to the door. Placing it against his right shoulder, he throws his body against the metal.

The steel sends painful vibrations deep into his bones, but he continues to crash against the door. The men watch in sorrow. They see how unforgiving the door is, and how relentlessly Tim tries. A few cannot bear the sight of his torment and turn their heads away.

Nevertheless, he still smashes his body into the metal. He does it over and over again without hesitation until the top hinge on the door bends sideways just a few millimeters. The other captives look at each other in disbelief. Tim breathes heavily as each blow bends the rusty hinges a little more until they begin to crack. The men's eyes widen in astonishment as with one final loud roar, he slams his shoulder deep into the fibers of the door, forcing it crashing down.

Tim lies on the ground, clutching his arm. He has cracked a bone in his shoulder. He manages to pull himself up and begins running between the huts, hidden by the night.

Two Nazis carry Emma down the halls of a dark

building, thrilled to have a prize in their clutches for the night. She screams hysterically, kicking and flailing against the men as she continues to cough. The soldiers just laugh and grip her tighter. They finally come to a large utility room and throw her inside. One of the soldiers starts clearing the area and setting up a table while the other one pulls at her hair and clothes as she tries to scurry away from him.

A single dangling bulb illuminates the room, but it is enough to show every tear on Emma's face. The man who has finished arranging the room drags her to the table. She scratches at him, coughing, and cries out, "Tim! Tim! No!"

The soldier twists both of her arms behind her back and slams her down on the table while she continues to kick. The other Nazi holds her legs down while pressing his hand heavily on her throat. Looking at her, he sticks his tongue out and begins to salivate. Then he unbuckles his uniform belt and caresses Emma's thighs with his hands, pushing up her torn skirt. Emma feels her arms and legs burn with exhaustion and her stomach turns. She feels the Nazi's rough palms on her thighs and tries with all her might to get away but the soldier behind her only presses down harder.

The Nazi's forest-green pants drop around his ankles in front of her. Unable to breathe, Emma starts to feel dizzy and begins to black out. With what little air she has left in her lungs she gurgles out one last cry, "Tim!"

As she screams the door flies open aggressively.

Its window shatters, sending shards of glass across the floor. Emma sees Tim charging towards her. He throws a punch at the Nazi who has his pants around his ankles, knocking him to the ground. Teeth fly from the man's mouth as he hits the wall and slides down, unconscious. The other man releases Emma and reaches for his gun. Tim lunges across the table, and the gun flies into a corner.

When the Nazi hits the floor, Tim starts to punch him relentlessly. The soldier grabs Tim's collar and is able to escape by flipping Tim onto his side. The Nazi pulls out a stag horn knife and tries to thrust it into Tim. He rolls out of the way and the Nazi sticks the blade into the wooden floor. Emma scurries to the wall in terror.

Tim looks for a weapon as the Nazi grabs him by the shirt. He wrestles free and throws a punch that just misses his opponent. When Tim swings, he winces in pain from the cracked bone in his shoulder. The Nazi wrestles him to the ground and pulls Tim into a choke, squeezing his arms in a vice grip. With all his strength, he pulls down on the Nazi's arms, trying to free himself. Tim's muscles strain until they tear under his skin. He feels himself becoming light-headed.

Emma looks around. She finds a piece of mending metal, picks it up and throws it at the soldier. It strikes his back with a thud, but he doesn't let Tim go. Emma throws other objects at him, screaming, "Stop! Stop it!" Her efforts are futile. Finally, she decides to run over to help Tim, but he waves her back, believing she will get hurt.

With a determined grimace, Emma raises another shard of metal, pivots her foot, raises her elbow, and twists her hips, throwing it directly into the back of the Nazi's head. It hits the target with savage force. The man releases Tim with a cry of pain. Tim pushes the Nazi off him and watches him move around, blind and screaming for help. Tim yanks the stag horn knife from the floor and strides towards the soldier, breathing heavily. Emma turns away. As he raises the blade, a gunshot goes off by the door.

Kaspar and four other soldiers stare in disbelief at the scene. Kaspar gives a command to Tim in German, to which he doesn't respond. The Nazi points his pistol at Tim and says, "Drop that."

Tim tosses the knife at Kaspar's boots. The Nazi holsters his gun. Looking at Emma, Tim assures her. "It will be alright."

Kaspar grabs Tim's throat, pushing him up against the wall as one of the other soldiers helps the blinded Nazi to his feet and leads him away. Another carries the unconscious soldier out. The remaining two prop up the fallen table.

Kaspar leans into Tim's face and hisses. Then he drags him to the table by the neck, slams him down and punches him in the stomach. Emma scurries over to the stag horn knife, picks it up and runs over to them, shouting and crying, raising the blade above her head. One of the soldiers strikes her across the face with his rifle, knocking her to the ground.

Tim screams, "No, Emma!" and tries to push

Kaspar away. The other soldier grabs him and shoves him backward.

Kaspar slicks back his hair and mockingly screams, "No, no, no!" and slaps Tim across the face. Emma looks up from the ground as her tears seep into the fresh cut across her nose.

Tim glances back at Emma. Kaspar watches the two look at each other and begins to laugh. The soldier who struck Emma helps pin Tim to the table. Laughing so hard he can hardly speak, Kaspar sputters, "Oh, that's right, this is why you have caused so much trouble! This is your woman! You are the American I took!"

Getting his laughter under control, he wipes his eyes and says, "Maybe I fix problem, eh?"

Kaspar reaches behind a box and grabs a hammer. "You are dog, American. You cannot keep you mind out of gutter with this one." He points to Emma, raises the hammer and screeches, "So maybe I smash what makes you dog!"

Tim struggles but the soldiers hold him too tightly. Kaspar grabs Tim's knee, pinching his fingers firmly into the tendons and pressing his leg against the top of the table. Tim bites his lip in agony. Kaspar raises the hammer high and laughs as he yells, "I told you I would show you hell, American!"

Emma screams.

The hammer falls fast, but Tim struggles out of its path. It strikes a muscle in his thigh and he groans in pain. Angry, Kaspar screams at his men to make Tim hold still. He raises the hammer and is about to swing again when a command echoes across the room. Everyone looks and sees Marcel standing in the doorway with the soldier who had helped the blinded Nazi.

"What is going on here?" Marcel yells angrily in German.

The soldiers offer blank stares. Marcel sees Emma on the floor but ignores her. In English, he says, "This is most unbecoming, Offiziere. We are not barbarians."

Marcel helps Tim up off the table. He then turns to Emma but acts surprised to see her there. Kneeling down, he asks kindly, "My dear, how badly are you hurt? Here, let me help you up." He extends his hand to her, and she allows him to help her stand. As Marcel moves to escort her out of the room Emma stops and says, "Wait." She looks at Tim and then back at Marcel.

Marcel pulls her to his side and says, "Please take the American back to his hut." The soldiers cuff Tim.

As Marcel leaves the room with Emma, Tim yells, "Marcel."

Marcel closes his eyes, annoyed by the ostentatious American. Then he turns around. "Yes?"

Tim says confidently, "In America, we have a saying for moments such as this... it goes 'Tonight, we gotta get git.'"

Emma's eyes widen.

"Captivating," Marcel sneers. He lets go of Emma and walks over to Tim. "You will see soon enough if it was God or the devil who brought you to my island." He then whispers to Kaspar, "Raupe."

"Tell your successor hello for me," Tim smirks.

Marcel leaves the room, grabbing Emma by the arm and taking her with him. Kaspar and the soldiers all smile as they pull Tim down the dim hallway.

When they arrive in Marcel's bedroom, he has draped a red cloth over a table in the center of the room. On the table lay several dishes of freshly prepared food. The sight and smells awaken hope and strength in Emma.

"I was enjoying dinner alone, but it would be a delight if you were to join me," he says.

Emma forces a smile. Marcel moves a chair to the table from the corner of the room for her. "Sit," he requests.

Emma joins him at the table as he waves his hand over the food and says, "Please." She resists at first but gives in to her hunger.

Marcel jingles out a pair of handcuffs and latches Emma's left wrist to her chair. "I want to be safe if I need to turn my back on you. You understand." Emma waits a moment, but then snatches an apple and chomps into it without any manners. Still chewing the apple, she reaches for a roasted chicken leg that steams when she tears it off. She chews voraciously before taking a gulp of water. Marcel watches her with a smile. "Slow," he says, "you might lose a tooth."

He snickers at his own joke as Emma continues to feast. He reaches under the table and pulls out a bottle of white wine. "Your dining won't be complete without a bit of formality, wouldn't you agree?"

Emma stops eating and looks at the bottle; she notices that the brand starts with a familiar-looking 'C.' The same 'C' she saw on her mother's wine. She immediately holds out her glass. "Yes... please." Marcel is thrilled with her cooperation and pours her a full glass. He pours himself a drink as well.

Out in the cold, Tim sees the bonfire blazing before a rag is tied tightly around his mouth as a gag and a black bag is flung over his head. He is forced forward until he reaches the great complex. Halted just a step away from the Raupe, he can hear men whimpering to his left and right. The smell of smoke mixing with the scent of the dead from the Raupe's last meal lingers in the air.

The icy wind stings Tim's bare skin and he tries to breathe slowly and deeply to calm his heart. A few minutes pass before a Nazi tears the black bag off of him and his head is shoved into a hole. The darkness blinds him as a metal clamp locks around his neck. The clamp is tight, but not suffocating.

Loud wailing and crying echo in his ears. The moldy air grows thicker and thicker. The cuffs come off his hands and, when the guards move on, he feels around his neck for any opening in the hole. He scrapes his fingers around the concrete and metal in desperation, trying not to panic. When he finds that he is almost able to fit the tip of a pinky finger through just under his throat, he reaches into his waistband and pulls out his blade of grass. Tim pushes the reed through the hole, sticking the blade into his good nostril. It works like a straw and he slowly breathes in clean air, still kicking his legs to act as if he is in peril.

Marcel brings out a third bottle of wine as Emma has three glasses to Marcel's six. She asks Marcel to dance. He smiles and stands her up from her chair, but when he does, her wrist snags on the handcuff. Emma looks down and frowns. Marcel ponders a moment with glassy eyes, then unlatches the cuff. Emma freely spins around. She is a small girl with barely any fat on her body, so it is no surprise to Marcel when she starts tripping over everything trying to dance. As she stumbles around, he walks over to his small wooden record player. With difficulty, he manages to place the needle onto the black vinyl. As the voice of Marion Harris fills the air, Marcel is caught up in the moment. "'After You've Gone,' an amazing American song... so beautiful!" He spins around, and there is Emma, ready to dance.

"Come now Monsieur Marcel, you mustn't leave me here to dance alone."

Marcel blinks to clear his blurry vision and smiles as he places one hand on Emma's hip. They twirl gracelessly around the room. When they bump into the table, Emma grabs the bottle of wine and takes a long swig. She offers it to Marcel and whispers, "Finish it for me."

Marcel almost drinks the bottle dry from her hand. When he can drink no more, he begins coughing, and Emma slips away. She grabs the pair of handcuffs and seductively approaches him to the rhythm of the music. He smiles in the candlelight as she play-fully pushes him onto the bed. She slowly chains one of his hands to the bedpost.

Marcel grabs her dress, pulls her to him and starts kissing her neck. She pushes away from his grip and stumbles to the record player to turn up the volume. He looks at her and slurs, "Come here."

Emma laughs and slowly walks back to him. She traces her fingers across his chin and lies down beside him. He rolls over to kiss her neck again. As he does, Emma whispers, "Know that you've made me feel much more pain than this."

In a flash, Emma yanks the stag horn knife from under her blouse and stabs it into his trachea. His eyes widen, and blood begins to stream from his neck. Emma closes her eyes and rolls onto the floor. He reaches for her but finds that he is still chained to the bedpost.

Marcel attempts to scream but emits only a low gurgle. Emma stands up, grabs the blankets and throws them into a pile against the wooden door. She finds two more bottles of wine which she empties onto the pile. She then rummages through the Hauptleute's dresser and adds some of his clothes to the pile while Marcel's blood soaks the bed. She grabs the phone but hears footsteps pounding down the hallway.

Emma puts on some of Marcel's clothes and packs the rest into a small bag before grabbing the burning candle from the table and igniting the pile by the door. Marcel's tugging at the cuffs grows weaker as his eyes begin to close. Smoke swirls inside the room as the tongues of fire hiss and crackle. Emma snatches Marcel's rifle from the corner. Crossing to the window, she bashes the glass out. Flames engulf the doorway, keeping soldiers at bay outside the room.

Fighting to survive in the belly of the Raupe, Tim hears the cries of the other men as they feel their guts wrenched from the inside. He keeps calm and breathes. He stays patient when the screams soften, and the men exhale their final breaths. A few minutes pass by while he remains in the silent emptiness of death. He can feel his face tingle from the gases and he keeps his eyes shut tightly so they will not be burned.

Latches eventually unhinge and the bodies are pulled out one by one. Light from the bonfire shines into the death chamber. Tim allows his body to go limp and motionless. When the truck for gathering bodies finally arrives, a Nazi unlocks Tim's head from the chamber and he falls to the ground, feigning lifelessness. Another soldier puts his body in a bag and tosses him onto the truck with the fresh corpses.

Tim counts the seconds in his head as the truck drives around the complex. The moment it reaches the end of the Raupe and turns, he whispers, "Now," and rolls off the bed of the vehicle to the ground. He waits for a moment to make sure no soldier has spotted him fall off. After the truck is gone, he wiggles his hands out of the bag and sticks his head into the cool night air. Making sure he is alone, Tim sneaks around to the dark building with his body bag in hand.

CHAPTER TWENTY-SEVEN

Watching frantically to make sure he is not seen, Tim races back to the other side of the island. He reaches Emma's hut, unlatches the lock from outside and swings the door open. All the women startle awake, shocked to see a man who is not in uniform. Instead, he is in rags, pale and panting.

"Emma!" he screams, as he rushes to her shelf and bends down. "Emma, I am..."

Tim drops to his knees in disbelief. Emma's shelf is empty. He rubs his hand where she slept, then runs a finger over the hole through which she whispered to him. He grabs her thin leather pillow and buries his face in it. Sobbing into the coarse cushion, he screams out of agony.

Tim stares hopelessly at all the pitiful faces in the walls. Suddenly he sees a figure step into the moonlit doorway. A large coated figure with thick pants stares at Tim, and then rushes toward him. He freezes as the figure advances rapidly. He no longer cares what fate holds for him without Emma.

When the silhouette reaches Tim, his eyes open wide when see Emma standing over him, dressed in men's clothing. They hold each other tightly, incapable of letting go. They sob, then grow quiet, but continue to hold each other in silence as the women watch.

"I'm sorry I wasn't in my hut."

Tim smiles as he pulls Emma away to see her face, and then he kisses her on the lips, pressing her body against his. She leans into his chest and cries while kissing him as if his lips quench a long thirst.

Tim grabs her hand to run outside. "Come, they will be after us!"

"Wait, I have some clothes for you." She reaches into the bag.

Tim shakes his head. "We can't use these. Not where we are going. They will bog us down. Strip to your rags."

Emma listens. They leave the remaining clothes on the ground and run. Tim leads the way to the open spot he left in the fence. He grabs the loose metal and pulls with all his might so Emma can crawl underneath.

Once she is through, he struggles to get himself under as well. The bottom of the fence tears his rags, and the rocks scrape his chest as he grimaces in pain. When he gets through, he digs by one of the fence poles and pulls up the rope from the crashed boat. "Right where I left you."

He grabs Emma by the shoulders and looks into her frightened eyes. "There are black, volcanic rocks down by the edge of the island. We need to grab as many as we can and throw them into this bag."

She nods.

The two run to the beach and search the ground. After a few moments, the bag is almost full. Tim ties the end of the rope around the top of the bag. He loops it around Emma's waist, securing it tightly before twisting it around his own waist in a knot. He wraps his arms around her. The chilling wind swirls around them as the choppy tide grabs at their feet.

Emma speaks into Tim's chest. "Will we make it?"

Tim lifts her chin up and looks into her eyes again. "Do you trust me?"

Emma nods and tears stream down her face. She looks over his shoulder at the island, seeing how much the fire she started has grown. Rubbing her arms, Tim instructs, "Now, whatever you do, don't let go of the bag. I will keep us facing south. All you have to do is kick."

He then takes her hands in his. "Do you feel how warm your hands are in mine?" She nods. "When we get into the water, just think of how your hands feel now; it will make the water feel warmer."

She embraces him one last time.

Tim asks, "Are you ready?"

Emma squeezes him tightly and answers, "Let's get home."

He holds her hand as they run into the water. Just a few steps into the sea and the water is hip-deep, forcing them to dive under. After accidentally gulping and gagging on the salt water, they grip the floating bag and begin to swim.

The freezing water nearly immobilizes them as they struggle to move forward. An agonizing chill tears at their skin, threatening to drown all thoughts of warmth and hope. Their teeth chatter uncontrollably. Tim swims with his good shoulder at first but as the cold numbs his body he is able to paddle with both arms. Emma tries her best to kick but rapidly grows exhausted and begins to drag. Tim continues to swim as best as he can. They work together until the island is out of sight and the dark body of water has them to itself.

High in the sky a streak of lightning explodes across the horizon, lighting the clouds. Thunder reverberates through the air as a storm hovers over the water. Clouds cover the stars and raindrops pour down on the two swimmers' heads. Ripples become waves and force them to swim harder, pushed sideways by new currents.

Tim yells, "Keep pushing, we are almost there!" even though land is completely out of sight.

The cold winds hurl water into Emma's face, gripping her with fear. The darkness of the storm now blocks out all light from the sky as waves drench them.

An occasional break in the clouds reveals the moon, which Tim uses to make sure they are headed in the right direction. He continues to encourage Emma as her movements grow sluggish, but the raging of the storm drowns out his voice.

The mysteries of the deep unleash towering waves behind the desperate pair. Tim feels his body recede backward as a mountain of a wave gets closer and closer. It peaks, then crashes down on their heads, throwing them both in a spiral under the water. Caught in the torrent, Tim loses his grip on Emma.

Eventually able to haul himself along the rope through the dark abyss, Tim grabs the floating bag again. He grips the coarse stones tightly as he spews water from his belly. Emma is not on the bag with him. Tim pulls on the rope until her body breaks the surface. She has blacked out from exhaustion.

Hoisting her up to keep her head above the surface, Tim kicks until his thighs burn. "Please let her be breathing," he shouts.

Suddenly, his calves cramp and every joint in his body locks up as saltwater floods into his mouth. Roaring waves drown out the thunder. His tense body grows sore. He fights to swim with all his strength, but his muscles are shutting down. Willpower yields to his spent, battered body, and he lets Emma slip from his grip into the water. He wants to pull her back up, but his muscles have forgotten how to respond.

The thrashing waters and rain beating at his face make it nearly impossible for him to open his eyes. Tim slowly begins to sink. The bag comes loose, and with one more wave it tears open, letting the porous rocks float freely in every direction. The sea slowly sucks Emma's body down.

Tim yells "No! God, No!"

Without the bag, the rope ties Tim to Emma,

who is like an iron anchor tugging him downward. He strains to stay above the water but feels his arms getting heavier and heavier as if he is trying to lift the sea itself. The suction of the current pulls Tim down until his face is all that bobs above the water. Each time he inhales, chilling water fills his lungs. He dips and rises in the saliva of the world but with every dip he stays under longer and longer until he ceases to surface at all.

Tim's wide eyes are intense under the water as panic begins to overtake his mind; he knows he is going to drown. He tries to thrash his way back to the surface to keep from dying, but it is useless. He flails in the freezing water as adrenaline pumps through his rapidly beating heart. His mind thinks futilely of ways to survive and then slowly darkens.

A strong wave suddenly yanks Tim and Emma to the surface, allowing him to inhale one last time. He sucks water and air deep into his lungs as he looks out over the sea. He is so dazed that he can no longer hear the roaring storm—he is numb. He feels his soul splitting from his body. Bloated grey clouds on a majestic royal blue horizon swim in the sky as rain cascades in sheets onto the surface of the whipping waters. Waves form like mighty soldiers from the depths, crashing into one another, then disappearing into the dark sea from whence they came.

Time stands still for a brief second until the wave crashes Tim down again, immersing him deeper than before. He looks up and watches the surface grow distant as he closes his eyes. For the first time in his life, he gives up. An undercurrent rips Tim's limp body below the waves. He is pulled by the will of the water and Emma's body follows without question. Even though Tim has given up, mercy finds him at the bottom of the unforgiving sea.

CHAPTER TWENTY-EIGHT

Out of nowhere, a force like no other picks up the storm and sucks it into the heavens. The battling clouds slow their flight and hang peacefully in the sky. The waters surge no more, and the creatures of the deep swim near the surface again while wild waves drift to sleep.

On the bottom, sea flora wave fearlessly as before. Clean air fills Tim's lungs. His eyes open only as slits while he becomes aware. He feels his body buried in murky sand as the tide sloshes against him, urging him to wake up.

He coughs up stagnant water from his gut and rolls over in the sand. He sees he has been washed up on shore. Realizing what has happened, Tim reaches for his waist and traces the rope. It leads to a spot above his head, where he sees his sleeping beauty lying peacefully on the shore with him.

Tim crawls over to her. "Emma. Wake, Emma. Please." He places his hands on her and presses her chest repeatedly with all his strength. Her lifeless face is a sign of Tim's failure. All he can do is hope she was breathing every time she surfaced. He inhales deeply, cupping Emma's mouth with his lips and exhales all the air in his lungs down her throat. He blows as if he is blowing the life in him deep into her. He pumps her chest over and over again.

After what feels like a lifetime, Emma chokes and gasps for air. She coughs so hard it seems her lungs will burst. Tim watches as tears of joy streak his sandy face. Then he scoops her into his arms while Emma blinks in disbelief, and then realizes they have made it safely to shore. She too cries, "We are safe!"

Soaking in the freedom, the two let their exhausted bodies rest in the wet sand and stare up into the night sky. Tim strokes Emma's hair before a faint noise seizes his attention. He pauses and listens hard. He sits up and scans the horizon, for it seems to be coming from out in the water.

Emma looks at Tim. "What's wrong?"

"Listen, do you hear that?"

"All I hear are the waves, Tim."

Tim squints to see what he is hearing, then leaps to his feet and grabs Emma's hand. "We have to go—now!"

Tim's panic startles Emma to her feet. They muster all the energy they can to sprint away. Emma turns around to see what frightened Tim. Kaspar and a small group of soldiers are landing in two motorboats.

Tim shouts, "The trees! Hurry!"

Her heart races with fear.

When they hit the tree line, Tim and Emma hear dogs howling and barking behind them. The Nazis are on the beach. Emma dodges tree limbs and thick bushes, trying not to let Tim's hand slip from hers. As they run, she sees a flashing light barely visible through the dense brush.

"Tim," she says, pointing, and he sees the light too. He utters, "The blue beacon... come on!" They rush toward the signal. They hear the dogs barking and growling, and with every passing second, the noises from the soldiers grow louder and louder.

"They are getting closer!" Emma cries.

Tim tries to think of what to do. "Why hasn't he let the dogs loose yet?" he asks under his breath. His mind stops. "He only wants me..."

Emma cannot understand what he says with the rustling of the forest.

"Dogs won't take his pride," Tim whispers to himself. Just then, he stops and pushes Emma up against a tree. "Climb!" he screams.

She ascends into the tree as Tim shoves her upward. He reaches into his trousers and pulls out a folded damp green sheet of paper, placing it in her palm.

"What are you doing?" she cries.

"Get to the blue light when it is safe," Tim says and clenches her hand tightly. He fights back tears when he sees her confusion. "I love you, Emma."

Tim lets go of Emma's hand and runs away, yelling and hollering to divert Kaspar's attention. Almost instantly, the growling dogs are set loose.

Emma screams, "TIM!!!"

The dogs sprint through the brush and jump on Tim, biting his arm and tearing into his skin. He yells and fights to keep them from ripping him to pieces. The soldiers catch up to the dogs and whistle them off. After continuing to chew on Tim's limbs for a few more seconds in disobedience, the dogs finally let go.

Tim pushes himself to his hands and knees and tries to stay up. Kaspar watches him for a moment before kicking him back to the ground.

"Pathetic," Kaspar smirks.

Two soldiers pick Tim up and pin him against a tree. Kaspar wipes his mouth and begins to beat him mercilessly. Tim strains not to yell. He knows Emma is close. She listens from the tree with her hand over her mouth. She is in shock, unable to move.

Eventually, Kaspar ceases his punches and his men let Tim drop to the ground. He pulls a pistol from his belt and places the barrel of his gun flush against Tim's head. There is silence for a moment, and Emma hopes Tim got away. Then she hears him scream, "FORGET ME!!!"

***

A loud bang goes off and Emma wakes up startled in her bed. Morning light drifts into the empty room. She presses a hand against her pounding chest and wipes sweat off her forehead with the cool sleeve of her nightgown. Getting out of bed, she grabs a coat and hat, and slips out of the bedroom, leaving a small note on her pillow. She closes the door silently so as not to awaken her husband.

After several minutes of walking, Emma sits down in the damp grass of a graveyard. Soft beams of light surround her as they pass through the quietly rustling trees. The breeze creates waves in her flowing golden hair as she holds her coat tightly around herself.

"You were with me in my dream last night." She chokes back tears. "I am still so sorry." She sniffles and wipes her nose with a handkerchief.

Emma's husband pulls to a stop on the road in a black Lincoln Phaeton with Leo in the front seat.

"Wait here, Leo," he quietly instructs as he steps out of the vehicle.

"I will never forget you, I can promise you that," Emma whispers as a pair of arms embraces her waist. She turns around.

"Hey, Beautiful."

"Tim! My goodness, you scared me! Where is Leo?"

"Leo is fine! He is waiting in the car." Tim wraps Emma in his arms. "I thought something was on your mind. You've been thinking of E, haven't you?"

"I have." Emma looks down. She pulls out a folded green sheet of paper and raises her face up toward Tim. "I don't say it enough, but you did provide for me, just like you said you would. I wish to thank you for that…"

She looks over her shoulder at the gravestone behind her. It reads *In Fondest Memory of Edeltraut "E" Abigail Roth*.

Tim allows Emma a few moments for one last

look at the stone. When she finally turns to him, he reaches for her arm, saying, "We are awfully blessed. Can't be grateful enough for those Swedes running to our aid."

Emma squeezes the folded paper in her hand.

Tim sees her hand and says, "What's this?"

"It makes me sad to think I almost lost you, too. I read it sometimes to remind me how blessed I am to have you."

"You know how much I wish you would toss that away. It makes me sad that you still read it."

"No, it does quite the opposite," she responds. "Would you?" She holds the paper up.

"Would I read it?"

"Yes," Emma says.

"Very well."

Tim unfolds the green paper with the word "Goodbye" across the top and begins to read.

To describe you is to describe love itself.
Love, a feeling stronger than all things else.
Like invisible cool pricks of sprinkled rain
As I walk along by Lake Stevens' side.

Immersion from under the light grey sky,
Bathed in you, I gaze to heaven with my eye.
Subtle aromas wafted from rich wet grass,
A loom of laughs as the spirits of spring fly.

Fresh dewy air that blurs my vision with tears,
You are why I can smile from ear to ear.

Though I am gone, and this paper is all that's left,
I will forever pray for you while I rest.
From Tim, with all my love

A honk comes from the street. "Mommy! Daddy! I want to go!" Leo shouts from the car.

"O, I almost forgot, we need to hurry." Tim explains. "They are coming to move our things in an hour." He takes Emma's hand to lead her back to the car, but she lets go.

"Just once more... please."

Tim grins with a nod and returns to the car alone.

Leo honks again. Emma turns back towards E's gravestone, kissing her hand and placing it on top. She walks a short way into the forest and finds a tree. Then she traces her fingers over its bark and gives it a soft kiss of its own.

She now heads back to the car, drying her tears as she walks. When she gets in the car, Leo asks, "What's wrong, Mommy?"

Emma smiles with teary eyes. "Nothing dear. Mommy is fine."

Tim looks back at her for a moment, then shifts the car into gear. Emma wipes her face and looks out the window as the car proceeds down the street. Through the trees she sees a crooked heart carved into the bark of a tree that reads, "Tim and Emma, Forever."

CHAPTER TWENTY-NINE

After turning off Padgett Road, Tim and Emma pull into the driveway of their new home. Leo swings open the passenger door. Emma waits a moment for Tim to make his way around the back of the car. He opens her door and takes her hand as she steps out. Hearing the car from inside the house, Tim's elderly mother opens the front door.

"Leo! Do you want to come help Grammy Wexford and me set up your room?"

"Yeah! I want to put my toys away!"

Emma smiles as she watches his little hand wrap around Tim's mother's fingers. All of a sudden, a familiar voice announces grandly, "The Andersons have arrived!"

Tim and Emma look over and see David Peace coming around the side of the house.

Tim teases, "Whoa, who invited you?" Dave laughs before giving Tim a hug, and then hugs Emma.

"Y'know, I just thought I'd come by and help, I knew you could really use these big guns." Dave dramatically curls his arms to flex his mediocre biceps.

"Yes sir! Everything you carry in is one less item I have to!" Tim laughs.

"Did Charlie make it up?" asks Emma.

"Unfortunately, no," Dave answers. "You know how busy he's been ever since he was elected Mayor of Seattle. But I'm sure when the moving part is done, he'll show up for your mom's home cookin'!" Dave laughs. "Come out back! I want to show you what I've been working on for the past week."

"Dave, have you really been out here working on the house all week?" Emma exclaims. "Goodness, you didn't have to go through any trouble like that."

Dave puts one hand on Tim's shoulder and the other on Emma's. "Listen, you two are my favorite people in the entire world. It's no trouble at all. Besides, it gets me away from the Mrs."

"You just got married a month ago and already need your space?" Tim laughs.

"Oh, no, she is great! I just thought we'd wait a while before trying to have a baby, but ever since you two introduced her to Leo, all she wants to do is have a kid. I swear I don't have the stamina for her."

Emma rolls her eyes, grinning. "And that's my cue to let you two head off. I'll come back around in a minute and see what you've done, Dave. I need to check on the movers." Tim and Dave head to the side of the house while Emma enters the front door.

"Emmeline!" Sarah cries, embracing her friend. "I was just in Leo's room helping the grandmothers out. I must admit, I wasn't sure about the move here.

It has fewer bedrooms. I thought a bigger home would be better so you and Tim could have more children."

"We'll see about that," Emma smiles, "but our old home will be put to good use by the city. The orphanage was running out of space. Tim and I are happy we could help."

"Well, Lord knows you two didn't have to give up your home. It seems like NOMA Electric is doing better and better every time I read the paper."

"We have Tim to thank for that. Everyone loves his lights."

Sarah's eyes grow wide. "Oh, you're not kidding! Would you ever have believed how popular they have become? Every year I think how much more beautiful Christmas is with them."

As Emma and Sarah catch up, Mr. Wexford walks by carrying a glass with clear liquid and a cube of ice.

"Father..." Emma raises her eyebrows and looks at his glass.

Mr. Wexford smiles and raises his drink, "It's water, Emmy. Can't an old man quench his thirst after moving his daughter's furniture all morning?"

Emma grins. Her father sips from his cup and walks on, grinning proudly. Emma steps aside to help direct the movers where to place everything as they walk in.

Tim and Dave stand at the edge of the sprawling back yard that overlooks the crystal blue waters of Lake Stevens. Tim squats to pick up a few rocks and slings them one at a time as they skip across the water.

"You sure built a mighty fine dock, Dave."

"Well, I had some help, but she did turn out fine. You now have the best dock of all the homes here, I'd say."

"Better than John Calhoun's lake house?"

Dave laughs. "Well, seeing how he lost everything for cheating Uncle Sam on his taxes, I'd say your dock is finer than all he was left with."

Tim chuckles, but his smile slowly disappears. He looks down at the cigar burn on his forearm, just above his serial number.

"You alright there, Anderson?

Tim stands up. "I've never told you this, but, when Emma and I were on that island... I thought a lot. One of the biggest things I thought about that kept me going was how disappointed you'd all be... y'know, if I ever gave up."

Dave reaches to shake Tim's hand, and then he pulls him in for a hug. "That's one thing you're not, Anderson, a quitter."

Dave notices Emma standing in the backyard. He motions her over to the dock. "Come have a look; she's sturdy!"

"I saw it from upstairs! It's beautiful. Thank you so much!" Emma gives Dave another big hug.

"Of course! Now if you'll excuse me, I think I saw some tea in the kitchen with my name written all over it!" Dave grins and turns toward the house.

Tim looks out at the new dock as Emma comes up and wraps her arms around him from behind. He places his hands over hers before spinning around to face her.

"Hey, Beautiful." Tim kisses Emma's forehead. She looks out over the still water. Tim gazes in the same direction.

Emma murmurs, "The water is so peaceful right now."

"I know what you're about to say, so don't say it."

Emma looks at Tim and laughs. "What do you mean?"

"You know what I mean."

Emma gives a quirky half smile, "I honestly am lost. I wasn't going to say anything more." She turns back to look at the lake.

"Oh, come now! You weren't about to say, 'I think now is a good time to teach you how to swim'?"

Emma giggles. "No, I wasn't going to say that!"

He raises his eyebrows, not accepting her innocent plea.

"But... that is a good idea!" Emma shouts and quickly tries to push Tim into the water. Tim spins around with a smile and lifts her up in the air.

"No! Tim! Don't!"

Emma plops with a splash. Tim had to step into the lake to toss her, so he is now wet up to his knees. Drenched, Emma throws herself onto Tim as he laughs and tackles him into the water. Falling at the edge of the lake, half of his torso remains on the beach with Emma lying on top of him.

Tim brushes Emma's wet hair from her forehead, "We're soaking. Let's get git'." He pushes to stand, but Emma stays on top of him.

"No," Emma says with a long kiss, "When I am with you, I am right where I need to be." Tim smiles and settles back down in the water. He holds her close as the sun shines rays of gold across the lake.

ABOUT THE AUTHOR

Matthew Sherman graduated from the
University of North Texas with a degree
in English, and a focus in Creative Writing.
From Tim is his first published novel.

Made in the USA
Middletown, DE
23 August 2020